STREET
OF
WIDOWS

STREET
OF
WIDOWS

& OTHER STORIES

Cassie Flint Fancher

GREEN WRITERS PRESS *Brattleboro, Vermont*

Printed in the United States

10 9 8 7 6 5 4 3 2 1

Green Writers Press is a Vermont-based publisher whose mission is to spread a message of hope and renewal through the words and images we publish. Throughout we will adhere to our commitment to preserving and protecting the natural resources of the earth. To that end, a percentage of our proceeds will be donated to environmental and social activist groups. Green Writers Press gratefully acknowledges support from individual donors, friends, and readers to help support the environment and our publishing initiative.

GReen
wriTers
press

Giving Voice to Writers & Artists Who Will Make the World a Better Place
Green Writers Press | Brattleboro, Vermont · www.greenwriterspress.com

ISBN: 978-1-950584-01-7

COVER DESIGN BY DEDE CUMMINGS & CASSIE FLINT FANCHER
The cover photo is of the author's great-grandmother, Elsie, and her pet sheep, Mabel, standing on the porch of their home in Barre, Vermont, circa 1903.

THE PAPER USED IN THIS PUBLICATION IS PRODUCED BY MILLS COMMITTED
TO RESPONSIBLE AND SUSTAINABLE FORESTRY PRACTICES.

Contents

STREET
OF
WIDOWS

In the House
Where I
Was Born

Coming Home, 2015

O UR HOUSE IS SMALL AND SET BACK FROM THE ROAD.
Just across the way is Lover's Lane, which curves
down the mountain and ends in a gravel parking lot in
front of what was once Rosalynn's Italian Restaurant.
These days the building is an affordable apartment com-
plex with only three apartments. None of the décor has
changed—cracked red paint on the walls, cheap gold
chandeliers, electric candles in the windows.

Up the hill, past the cemetery and the lumber mill, is
the main part of town. It isn't much, just a couple of brick
buildings with their backs to the river. The General Store,
Snap's Diner, Sip n' Suds Coffee Shop and Laundromat. In
some of the neighboring towns, gentle flow yoga studios
and cafes with poetry painted on the walls have begun to

crop up. Not here. On the other side of Main Street there is a hardware store and a supermarket. Behind the buildings, the river presses in tight. Trees drag their roots in the water and moss covers the ruins of an old mill and coffin factory, burned down back in the 1940s. At the entrance to one of the buildings, a set of cement steps still stands. Kids go there for their first kiss, their first cigarette, their first everything. Used needles litter the ground.

In the fall, the air is thick with sulfurous smoke. When winter comes, scratching red spots into people's cheeks, the needles freeze in the mud and are covered with clean snow. The river turns to ice as it runs.

Chicken Coop, 1991

When he was first married, my father put up a chicken coop behind the garage. He said he dreamt one night of a great hen that strained and crowed, laying smooth round eggs that cracked open, revealing his wife to him in pieces: scalp, tongue, toenail. In the morning he went to work, nailing together old boards and sealing up the cracks with thick paste.

He worked for three days, putting in mesh wire and heat lamps. When he was done, he brought my mother out to see. They crawled inside the crooked archway, bodies pressed close. The air was thick and made their skin wet. He touched his wrist to the back of her knee, moved closer to take her face in his hands.

That was the afternoon that Oscar was conceived, my mother always said, deep in the muck of the chicken coop. The rain turned the backyard yellow and green.

"We'll raise chickens," my father said when they were done. "We'll raise chickens and in the mornings we'll collect their eggs." But in the end there was never any time for that.

Winter of Rice, 2002

After the news came about my father, my mother stopped cooking anything but rice. She made it in the afternoons, letting the water boil over, using no salt. It was waiting in the fridge when Oscar and I came home from school, packed into the block shape of a Tupperware. "I can't eat anything else," she said.

Oscar bought us sandwiches at the store and showed me how to mix the rice with water to make a paste that we mashed into the wooden kitchen table. He made it a game. "This is how glue is made," he said.

Mother, Father, 1989

Once, they took the train all the way from Castleton to Penn Station for no reason at all. They'd driven to the Castleton station, decided on the way where to go. The station had worn wooden beams and patterned quilts on the walls. The stationmaster made them cups of Lipton black tea and asked where they were going.

"New York," they said. Neither of them had ever been.

They napped on the train, her head on his shoulder, his head on top of hers. The train rattled past the backs of houses, through passageways cut into deep black rock. They woke up when they were only halfway there.

"How tall do you think the buildings will be?" she asked.

He shrugged. "I heard you can't look up," he said, "or else they'll know you don't belong."

From Mother, 2001

We could never agree on how we met. "Through a mutual friend," my husband said. I thought it might've been at the post office. We used to send so many letters. He would decorate the envelopes he sent—triangles and squares and tiny scratch marks around my name like confetti.

It was eight months before he so much as held my hand. We were standing at the edge of the forest. "Listen for owls," he said, sliding his hand into my mitten. White wings beat among the dark branches. He moved to stand behind me, holding me until I stopped shivering. His chin was sharp against my shoulder, breath hot on my neck.

The night my husband said he was leaving, I would not let him touch me. We cried on opposite sides of the bed. In the morning, he woke to find me sketching him sleeping. I didn't want to talk, but I put my fingertips up to his cheek and left them there. We lay in bed and listened to the radio in silence. It was the same story again, the same news.

"I have to go," he told me.

The Attic, 2001

Before my father went to war, he painted the attic rainbow colors. It was a sloppy paint job, red and purple triangles that dripped down against a yellow background. He took the family photos stacked in boxes and hung them on the walls to make room for our toys. We had a little orange slide and a cracked trampoline where Oscar brought the G.I. Joes and naked Barbie dolls to battle. When they died, he let their bodies bounce to the floor.

The day my father left for war he spent the morning in the attic, painting more triangles. He kept mixing new colors. "This is fuchsia," he said, and another triangle would go up. "Here look, this is called chartreuse." He painted hundreds of triangles, some as small as the pupil of my eye. He painted until my mother called us down for a last lunch, until it was time for him to say goodbye.

When my father didn't come home, one of our elderly neighbors, Mrs. Bixby, began dropping by to check on us. She threw out the spoiled rice in the fridge and made sure that Oscar and I were still taking baths. One day she went into my parents' bedroom and boxed up all of my father's things. She went into the closet, took his clothes from the hangers, and shook them so the smell came out. My mother lay in her bed and said nothing. My father's things were boxed and brought to the attic. They stood in towers, smelling like cedar mothballs, casting shadows on the colorful walls. Oscar and I stopped going up there. The neighbor lady even packed up our CDs and put them away. She said that sound could trigger memories and that was the last thing we needed.

Four years later, Oscar found our father's gun up there among the boxes. He didn't tell anyone, just tucked it away in the drawer of his nightstand and allowed himself to feel mighty while he slept. He took me into his bedroom once and told me, "If I'd gone to war, I would've come back." I asked him how he knew. "Don't be stupid," he said. "I would've come back."

From Mother, 2002

I am alone in the dining room when I hear the knock on the door. I imagine his last breath at the exact moment I hear the news, though I know that isn't how it works, that he's been gone for hours, maybe days. The mid-afternoon sun lights the dust particles in the air. Someone told me once that even now we are breathing in molecules of Julius Caesar's last breath. I breathe deep, trying to inhale my husband's molecules. My throat catches and nothing goes down. The food in my stomach feels cold and heavy, like I've swallowed his corpse.

I don't want to be home, so on Sunday I drive to church. I leave the children behind. We've never been to church before and I'm in no mood to explain God to them.

The inside of the chapel is full of the same dusty light as my dining room. It makes shapes on the floor and on the side of the priest's round, pockmarked face. The walls are plain and there is only stained glass in one of the windows, but the priest has an engraved golden Bible that he props against the podium, angled so the cover catches the light and sends it bouncing back into the congregation.

"If God exists," my husband always said, "he sure as hell doesn't live in a church."

The woman next to me smells like canned tomatoes. She has her thin white hair fluffed up and lavender eye shadow applied in thick swoops across her eyelids. She knows all of the words to the mass and looks at me when I miss an "amen."

I wonder how my husband looked when he died.

There is a wooden crucifix on the wall. Jesus's body is contorted, but his face has been sanded smooth. His fingers hang down, nails in his palms. I am not sure exactly why I'm here. I try to recall the details of his resurrection.

The woman next to me reaches for my hand. I take it. Her skin is dry and her fingers bony. "Peace be with you," she says. All across the congregation, people are doing the same.

"I'm new here," I whisper, hoping she will understand. "I don't know what to say. My husband—"

Her thumb rubs slow circles on the inside of my palm. I can't stop staring at her lavender eyelids.

That night, I dream that she is speaking into my ear. "I pull out my hairs and leave them in sacred places."

Even in the dream, I am not sure how to respond.

"Try it," she says, and leans over, pulls out a single strand of my hair, and lets it float to the ground in a ray of light. It twists and curls around the dust molecules. Her tomato paste smell is not so bad. "You're a part of it now," she says, and turns back to the priest and the altar. Outside, the sun goes behind a cloud and the light turns gray. The shapes on the floor disappear. The dust moves through the air of the church, brushing against my skin, invisible as breath.

Elvis, 2003

Elvis came to town during the winter of my fifth-grade year. It was the winter after Dad died. The winter of the rice. Elvis drove into town in a beat-up white Mustang with "4 Elvis" engraved on the plates, wearing mirrored sunglasses and a leather jacket. No one knew how he'd ended up here, so far from Memphis, so far from anyone he knew or claimed to know. He was older than I'd expected, with wrinkles around his mouth. I saw him in the gas station, sometimes in the park. He was always drinking Coca-Cola. He paid extra to drink it from a glass bottle.

Oscar said not to talk to him. Elvis was dead, he told me, and Coca-Cola was better out of the can.

I didn't tell Oscar, but sometimes Elvis waved to me in the park. I waved back. One day I went up to him and told him that Elvis was dead, just in case he didn't know. He took off his sunglasses and looked me straight in the eyes. I was bundled up in a coat and a thick wool scarf, but he kept his leather jacket unzipped. His voice was so low I had to lean close to hear him over the wind.

"That's what they want you to think, kid," he said.

"I heard Elvis died on the toilet," I said.

He shook his head. "Don't listen to all that. You think a voice like that can ever die?" He hummed a section of "Blue Suede Shoes" for me, eyes closed.

My father used to sing Elvis songs sometimes. He would walk around the house humming, and when he caught sight of Oscar and me he'd move in close and belt the words in our ears, breath hot and face smelling of shaving cream.

Elvis told me he was next in line for the Presley fortune—or had been until some second cousin butted in and took what was his. He was still waiting for his money. Until then, he said, his whole life was dedicated to his family.

Oscar said that Elvis was stupid for waiting around in this town for a family that wouldn't come.

Elvis showed me the tin of black grease in the glove compartment of his car. He was always running it through his hair with a pocket comb, asking how he looked. "I'm Elvis," he would say, wiping the frost off his side-view mirrors to give himself a wink.

I didn't ask questions. There were days I still caught Oscar wearing Dad's old shirts, face smelling like Barbasol.

Memory of My Living Room, 2009

My mother painted the living room white the summer after Oscar crashed the truck, the summer after he went to jail. She worked all day, radio tuned to a broadcast about the fish in the local lake, part of a statewide water conservation series. Sweat dripped down her face and soaked through in a patch between her shoulder blades.

"Fish can't close their eyes," she told me after the first coat, taking a break out on the front steps. "Can you imagine? They see everything. Can't even look away." She wiped her palm across her forehead, closing her own eyes and squeezing them shut.

The paint was cheap and badly stirred, drying thin in some places and thick in others. She had moved the photographs from the top of the piano to protect them. They lay face up in the center of the floor: my parents' wedding day, me at my sixth-grade piano recital, Oscar as a newborn, red and wrinkled, still easy to love.

It was dark by the time the second coat went up. An ad for windshield replacement was playing through the static.

"Did you know," my mother asked me, "that catfish carry their eggs in their mouths for weeks while they wait for them to hatch? The fathers do. They don't eat the whole time."

"No, I didn't know."

The photographs were still on the floor, and she stood over them for a long moment, chest rising and falling with her breath, nostrils dilated, eyes closed. Oscar's baby face looked up at the shadows on the ceiling, laughing.

"You were such a lovely piano player," she said finally, eyes blinking open, unfocused.

The Truck, 2000

Dad's truck was red with a white stripe and rust flaking off down around the wheels. There was only one row of seats, so even when I was small I got to sit up front and look out the windshield at the road sliding away beneath us. There was a switch for turning the passenger-side airbag on and off. Dad kept it turned off. He said if the airbag deployed, even just for a minor crash, I could suffocate and die.

Dad did all kinds of tricks when he drove. He'd take both hands off the wheel and drive with just his knees. He'd put an old tape in, turn the volume way up, and jerk the wheel around like he was being possessed by the music. Sometimes, on an empty stretch of road, he'd take Oscar or me on his lap and let us steer while he worked the pedals. Afterwards, he'd give us a stick of cinnamon gum from the glove compartment. "Nice work," he'd say, suddenly serious, eyes fixed on the road ahead. He always chewed two sticks of gum at once. Because he was bigger, he said. Same reason he had to take the wheel from us when the road curved around the banks of the river.

From Oscar, 2008

When I turned sixteen, I pulled the tarp off of Dad's old truck and started on repairs. The tires were worn through and the water pump was pretty shot too. All my savings went towards new wheels, but I was still stuck with the leaky pump. I got myself a job unloading delivery trucks and stocking shelves at the supermarket in town. It didn't pay much, but I opened a savings account and put away most everything I earned. In the meantime, I carried around a gallon of water in the bed of the truck. When the coolant started to leak and the engine overheated, I'd just pop the lid, let the whole thing smoke, and then pour a little cool water in to get everything running smoothly again.

I met Lisa at the supermarket. She worked register 6, the express lane, her favorite. She had a picture of her baby taped up. "That's Lucy," she'd say, pausing with a cucumber in her hand to point out the photograph. "She can say 'Ma' now. Oh, she's a smart one." Lisa was a little older than me—twenty-two—with watery eyes and short blond hair that she kept smoothed down flat over her ears. I was lining up boxes of raisins the first time I saw her, and what came into my mind was how her toes might look after a long, hot bath.

Lisa lived in a three-room house behind the cemetery. She kept it bright white, forever trying—and failing—to layer over the word "SLUT" that someone had spray-painted in tall blue letters. A bad breakup, she told me.

She never kissed me, but sometimes she let me take her to the movies, riding shotgun in the seat of Dad's truck, Lucy's car seat jammed in between us.

From Oscar, 2008

"You can hold my hand if you want," Lisa told me on the day we cremated her dog. She and I were standing on a patch of scrubby grass in her backyard, me kicking my toes against my heel and trying not to look at her big, stiff collie, Leo. There was still dirt in the cracks between his paws, like he'd been digging something deep.

"Okay," I said, taking a quick peek at her face to see if she'd been crying. She hadn't. I took hold of her hand, sort of snatching at her fingers, but let go right away, remembering my dried, cracked-up skin and the two warts on my ring finger. "I brought the lighter fluid," I said, shrugging my backpack off my shoulders.

"You do it," she said, so I uncapped the bottle and poured the fluid all over Leo's matted fur while Lisa watched. She still wasn't crying, but I didn't know if she was breathing either. I pulled my lighter out of my pocket and squatted down near Leo's narrow face. The skin of his eyelids had been tugged down over his eyes. I put the flame to his fur, watched it spread down the fluid on his spine and go up in a blaze. It took every ounce of my self-control to stay standing there, with bits of flaming fur falling from Leo's body and the smell of his burning flesh. Lisa's eyes were watering now, but mostly from the smoke. "Thank you," she told me, so quietly it was as if she was talking to God or someone else she didn't really believe was there.

From Oscar, 2009

Lisa was riding shotgun in my truck. She was touching my leg. The flavor of her perfume burned the back of my throat. I breathed deep, tried to swallow the feeling and keep it inside.

"You're the closest I have to a family, you know," she said. Her eyes were half closed, her limbs spread. I couldn't keep my eyes on the road. It had begun to rain. Fat, dark drops glistening at the edges of the windshield.

"We could be," I said. "We could be a real family."

Lisa didn't respond, just passed me the whiskey from where it was lodged between her leg and Lucy's car seat.

It was nearly empty. We'd been drinking all afternoon, finishing the bottle bit by bit. My stomach felt hot, full of sour liquid. I took a long swig, my throat burning. "Lisa . . ." I wanted her to feel that burn, to reach inside me, to grasp the warmth in her hand and make it hers.

"You're always mine," she was saying.

My arms were shaking. I turned to look at her. "I'm always yours."

"Oscar," she said, but she was slurring her words now, eyes closed. Her head nodded to the side and her mouth fell open just enough to show the pink of her tongue.

I took a hard left and Lucy woke with a scream. Lisa jerked upright. She undid the buckles and took her daughter from the car seat, bouncing her on her knee and making little noises until the screaming stopped.

"Touch her hair," she said. "It's like mine."

I reached over and felt Lucy's tuft of thin, blond hair. Then I reached farther and my fingers were in Lisa's hair, soft and thin against the heat of her scalp.

"Do you remember the day your father died?" she whispered. She reached back and untangled my hand from her hair, holding it on her lap against the warm inside of her thigh.

"Of course," I said. "I was in the playroom when we found out. My sister came upstairs and told me, 'Mama is throwing up in the bathroom.'"

Lisa passed the bottle again. I took another long drink, heat rising into the back of my throat. I turned the car left, headed up the mountain and back towards town. My vision kept getting darker, darker, as if there were no light anywhere. I blinked hard, trying to focus on the black shine of the pavement. Things were moving too fast. Lisa's perfume was mixing with the whiskey and it all burned. So hot I thought I might be sick.

"What are we doing?" she asked. "Let's go home."

My head was too heavy to nod. We were drifting across lanes, across time. My father was in the truck with us, chewing cinnamon gum. Lisa was asleep again, her neck curving towards my shoulder. Lucy was still in her lap, sleeping with her body nestled into the space between Lisa's legs.

"Lisa," I said. "Lisa. Lisa."

She didn't wake up. I reached for the bottle, took one more sip. The road began to straighten out near the falls. I couldn't see town yet, but I knew we were coming up on it, coming up on the grocery store and the laundromat. I imagined I was inside the laundromat, with the warm yellow lights, and Lisa separating her clothes into three different washers. My arms felt heavy, like I was holding the detergent for her, like she had her hand on my wrist while I poured and she was smiling up at me.

Crash, 2009

Oscar didn't remember the rest, but it wasn't hard to piece it together. His eyes closed. The truck angled to the right, began to pick up speed. They lurched forward, over the bank.

Lucy's skull cracked against the windshield. Dead on impact. No time to cry. The bottle shattered. Bits of glass lodged in the soft parts of their skin.

Elvis, 2009

Elvis saw me in the park late that summer, the summer of the crash. He had his car parked in the shade of a maple tree and he offered me a cigarette when he saw me. "I read what happened in the papers," he said. "It's been all over the headlines."

I sat with him on the hood of his car for a bit, watched the stoplight at the intersection change colors. Elvis told me he had a lead on the second cousin who'd stolen his fortune.

"It's not about the fortune," he said. "That's my family legacy I'm talking about."

I took the cigarette. "Do you ever get tired of waiting for your family?"

Elvis tugged a tuft of his chest hair out from underneath his shirt collar and looked away from me, across the street, shaking his head. "You still don't get it," he said. "I'm not waiting for anybody at all." He hummed a little. "Heartbreak Hotel." "I'm Elvis," he said to me, like there was nothing else for him to say, like if I didn't understand him by now, there was nothing he could do for me.

SHEEP WOMAN

For their honeymoon, Jack used his savings to rent a cottage on Chincoteague Island. There were wild horses, he said, like the Rolling Stones song. "Childhood living is easy to do," he sang and pulled Leanne up out of her chair to swing her around in a circle. He'd gotten a deal on a beachfront location, a little beige house with peeling paint and a driveway made of crushed clamshells.

Jack drove almost the whole way down, Leanne fiddling with the radio dials and humming snippets of songs, watching his slow, steady blinking as he kept his dark eyes fixed on the road. In the trunk, packed in beneath Leanne's underwear—the new ones with the red and white lace—was a gallon-sized freezer bag full of Mabel's ashes. She had sealed the top, and then taped it too, just to be safe.

Mabel had come to Leanne as a tiny gray lamb, still wet from the womb. She was born backwards, killing her mother in the process. Leanne was only nine years old, and it was her first time taking care of something that needed her. She would sneak baby Mabel into the bed at night, keeping her warm in her arms and waking periodically to feed her milk from a baby's bottle.

When they grew up, Leanne planted Mabel an alfalfa garden. Mabel's favorite time to eat was when it was raining, or had just rained, and she could stand in the garden with her hooves sunk deep in the mud.

They pulled up to the cottage just before seven in the evening. Jack left Leanne to unpack their things while he went out to pick up some beer.

There was a big wooden anchor hanging above the kitchen sink. She opened the cooler first and put some things in the fridge. All they had were a couple of apples and the cheese sandwich she hadn't eaten for lunch. She set the cooler by the door, then picked up the larger bags to bring them upstairs. Hers was heavier than Jack's— because of Mabel's ashes, she supposed.

At the top of the landing, Leanne heard footsteps on the back deck and the sound of a man she didn't know clearing phlegm from his throat. She tensed and looked behind her, almost went back downstairs to see who it was but decided against it and brought the bags into the master bedroom. Jack would be home soon anyway.

She unzipped her suitcase and took the ashes out. She didn't want him going through her things and finding them. Leanne looked around for a place to hide the bag, but the house was so clean that there weren't a lot of options. Finally, she took her raincoat out of her suitcase and wrapped it around the ashes. She stuck it on the top shelf of the closet and put a towel over it, and her swimsuit, which she wasn't likely to use. Then she zipped her suitcase back up and slid both bags under the bed.

Downstairs, there was a knock at the back door. Leanne tried to look out one of the upstairs windows, but there was an awning over part of the back deck and she couldn't see a thing. The knocking sounded again. She closed the door of the bedroom as quietly as she could and tiptoed downstairs.

It was the man they had rented the house from. He lived next door.

"Can't get the hot tub to work," he said.

"Oh," she said, and added, "My husband will be home soon."

The man nodded, like he didn't care all that much. "Anyhow," he said, "I tried to get it working but it's not happening so I'll just have to deduct from your bill. Sorry about that."

Leanne told him it was no problem and then closed the door and stepped back into the house. It was getting dark outside, and as he walked away the man triggered an automatic porch light that made her jump.

When Jack came home with the beer, he cracked open a bottle and poured a glass of water for Leanne. She was happy to see him—being in new places made her nervous—and kept taking his hand in both of hers and pressing her thumbs deep into his palm. They went out on the deck and sat, drinking in the sunset, watching the cold green water gurgle in the bottom of the hot tub.

"It's good to be here," Jack said, and Leanne agreed, it was as good as anywhere.

Leanne had been a bartender when she met Jack, because the money was good and because she liked having her mornings to herself. The pub she worked at was vaguely Irish themed, called O'Hare's even though the owner was a man named Charlie Young who was not Irish and who would tell you, if you bothered to listen, that his ancestors had been in Vermont since the time the Mayflower came over. Sox fans since the invention of baseball, he'd add, holding up his hand in assurance.

There had been a game on. She could remember because a man had been asking her to turn it up, turn it up, could you please turn it up some more? And when she'd told him that no, she was very sorry but she couldn't do that, the man had knocked his beer glass onto the floor and walked out. By the time Leanne got out front with the broom, Jack was already crouched on the floor, his black hair hanging in front of his eyes, holding the biggest shards of glass in his palm. One of his fingers was bleeding. "Guess I made more work for you," he said when Leanne had to take him out back to get him cleaned up.

She put a paper towel into his bloody hand. "You have to press hard," she said, "to get it to stop bleeding."

Leanne spent her first Chincoteague morning in bed. Jack read to her from brochures he had picked up at a rest stop. "Listen to this," he said. "Some people say the ponies are descended from survivors of a Spanish shipwreck."

"Who are some people?"

"Some people who wrote this brochure." He chuckled.

When it was nearly noon, he left the house and came back with a box of donuts, which she ate under the covers, listening to the rain and getting frosting on the sheets.

When the rain let up, the two of them went out for a walk, past shops with boogie boards and horse figurines in the windows, past seafood stands and rows of crooked little homes painted lavender and yellow. On the corner, a few blocks down, was an old, whitewashed church with kids learning to ride their bikes in the empty parking lot. They moved in circles, yelling back and forth, one girl daring the others to leave the driveway and head out onto the open road while she hung back behind the pink buds of a crepe myrtle tree.

When they got hungry, Jack and Leanne stopped in at an all-you-can-eat place called Crabs. "I Got Crabs on Chincoteague Island," the T-shirts said in big white block letters. "Hilarious," Jack said when he saw the shirts and stopped the nearest server to ask for the price. "It's our honeymoon," he said. "Any special deals for a couple of newlyweds?"

Mable had lived a long life. Leanne spent Mabel's last several years in a constant state of anxiety over Mabel's advancing age, checking her tongue for spots and feeling her sides for tumors. Sometimes her heart clenched and she had to close her eyes, sending one-word prayers into the universe. *Immortal, immortal, immortal.* When Mabel finally did get sick, Leanne felt a sense of calm, of things being as she had always expected them to be.

At sunset, they went down to the beach and sat on the wet sand. It was April, and the sea spray was still sharp with cold. Leanne found a spotted pink crab shell and held it flat in her palm to get a closer look. Its edges were lined with spikes and two small holes for eyes. She imagined how it might have moved across the ocean floor, clinging tight to the bottom, getting tossed up and overturned by the tide. Jack reached over and took the shell from her, made it scuttle along her leg, up her thigh, onto her stomach.

"I got crabs on Chincoteague Island," he said and laughed into the gathering darkness.

Leanne put a hand over Jack's to stop the shell's progress, letting it rest on her stomach. The tide was coming in and the waves, when they crashed, shot foam up onto Leanne's shoes.

"You'll be a good mother," he told her. His hand was still pressing her stomach. She thought of Mabel's cloven hooves. Of Jack's finger split open and bleeding on the night they'd met.

Growing up, Leanne had cut off snips of Mabel's wool and played with them like dolls. She'd made the dolls by looping the wool around her finger, tying it off with string to make the head, letting the wispy extras hang low like a dress. She called them her sheep women, and they slept lined up on her dresser.

Sometimes Mabel tried to eat the sheep women, chewing them with a look of distaste, like she recognized her former wool. Still, Mabel was Leanne's best playmate. She let Leanne cuddle her like a doll, brush her, tie ribbons to her ears. She listened to secrets without blinking, her black, horizontal pupils narrowed in thought.

About a week after Jack cut his finger, he came back to the bar asking for Leanne. "Just wanted to let you know I'm all healed up," he said, showing her the puckered skin stretching inward across the cut.

"Looks like it'll scar," she said, taking his palm into hers and turning it over.

He held her hand then, across the bar. "Leanne," he said. "It's Leanne, right?"

She smiled. "Good memory."

"I'm Jack," he said, and she could feel his new skin pressing into her palm.

They had only been seeing each other for a few months when Leanne found out she was pregnant. She had taken the test at work, and when she left the bathroom, Jack was there, squinting up at the beer menu on the wall. He smiled and waved her over.

"When are you off?" he asked. "I was thinking I could come over tonight." He reached across the bar and circled his hand around her arm, like he was holding onto her.

Leanne shook her head. "No," she said. "No, maybe not tonight."

When Jack stayed over, Mabel had to sleep on the floor. "Most sheep sleep in barns, you know," he'd said once when Leanne told him how cold the floor could get at night.

When she told him about being pregnant, he proposed, the scar shining on his open, empty palm. There hadn't been time for rings, he explained, as though she might not understand how fast the whole thing was happening.

"No," Leanne said. She shook her head. "You hardly know me."

"I know you," Jack told her. He was breathless and his cheeks were pink. She thought he looked like a child at the top of a slide. "I know you like dark beer and donuts with chocolate frosting," he said. "I know you can patch up a cut. I know you love seashells and classic rock. I know you'll be a great mother."

Leanne was annoyed that he didn't take her rejection more seriously. "I'll think about it," she told him. She went home to Mabel, who was lying on her bedroom floor, joints swollen and arthritic. There was urine leaking out from between her hind legs.

"Mabel," Leanne had said. "Mabel, Mabel, Mabel." After she'd mopped the floor, she'd slid both hands beneath Mabel's matted wool and helped her into bed. She warmed some milk in a bottle. When Mabel was done drinking, Leanne pulled the comforter up around them both so only their chests and heads were exposed.

"I'm pregnant," Leanne said. Mabel picked her head up off the pillow and blinked slowly, working her jaw as though she were chewing. Then she dropped back down to nuzzle in Leanne's armpit.

Mabel died that night, with her chin resting on Leanne's outstretched wrist. Leanne imagined she had made it until sunrise, but she really couldn't be sure.

In the afternoon, she called Jack.

"Decide yet?" he'd asked. He sounded chipper, she thought. Chipper.

"Mabel died at sunrise," she told him.

"Oh."

"It's okay."

"You're okay?" he asked.

"Yes." Mabel was still in bed next to her, gray wool hanging in tufts across her closed-up, crinkled eyes. "I'm saying yes, let's get married," she said, and then she hung up the phone before she could change her mind.

They were married that weekend, down at the courthouse.

At night, the rental house creaked and moaned. Jack's body was cold and clammy against hers. *I got crabs on Chincoteague Island*, she thought. When he leaned over and began rubbing at her thigh, she closed her eyes. She tried to remember the song. *Wild horses couldn't drag me away.* He moved his hand up over her stomach and onto her breasts. *Wild, wild horses . . . couldn't drag me away.* She thought of the Ziploc bag of ashes wrapped up in her raincoat and her towel. When he moved his hand back down, across her other thigh, she opened her eyes and slid beneath him.

On her second morning in Chincoteague, Leanne woke before Jack. She used the downstairs bathroom to be sick. She liked to be private about those things.

She took Mabel's ashes, still wrapped in her raincoat, packed them into the cooler, and left the house as quietly as she could. She followed the thick scent of salt and mud down to a wooded area by the beach. There was a gravel trail that led off into the trees for a few yards before splitting three ways. Leanne chose the path all the way to her right and followed it through the trees, still wet with dew, until the gravel turned to wooden slats that led out to an elevated lookout platform. She made it to the railing, then set down the cooler.

The land beneath the platform was muddy and wet, with green and yellow reeds growing close together, tangled, like thick underbrush. Four or five white birds flew between the reeds. The word *egret* came to Leanne, though she couldn't be sure that it was accurate. Across the reeds, where the ground became drier and sandy, were the wild horses. They stood together in a group, not doing much of anything. Leanne had hoped for them to be long and lean, running free on the open plains, but these horses had thick legs and long, matted hair, and they kept very still, with their black and white heads nosing the salty ground.

Leanne looked again and could see that a thin wire fence had been strung about halfway between her and the horses. The bulk of the wild horses, she had read, lived on the neighboring island of Assateague. Maybe they ran free there, galloped down the beaches, put their hooves in the water, snorted stinging salt water up the nostrils of their leathery noses. Maybe she was looking at the wrong horses.

She bent down and opened the cooler, unwrapped the freezer bag, stuck her fingers into Mabel's ashes. Soft and cold, like sand dug from deep beneath the earth. She took a handful and held it out to the wind. Ashes blew into the green reeds, damp from sea spray and dew, then stuck, turning the reeds a whitish gray. She reached for another handful. She thought again of Jack's bleeding finger. *Press it hard so the bleeding will stop.* She did not know how to take care of a baby. Did not know how to take care of a husband. Mabel's ashes were blowing in the wind and none of it mattered, not really. She was a sheep woman now, and all her parts were wisping away.

SOCKS

ON THE THURSDAY NIGHT AFTER LEO CRASHED his motorcycle into the side of a semi, Jenny washed his socks in the sink and tried to think about his death like he'd moved to another country that she might some-day visit. She would book her flight—a window seat— and on the airplane, she would order a glass of red wine. It would come in a plastic cup and she would take small sips to make it last.

She was using peppermint soap, and it made her nose itch. The socks were black, and in the dim kitchen light she couldn't see any stains, but when she rubbed in the soap the suds turned red and brown, and little flecks stuck under her fingernails. She squeezed more soap onto her hands and rubbed and rubbed until the bubbles foamed white. She thought about what she might pack on her trip. Travel-sized toothpaste, a thick sweater, Leo's clean socks.

The whole thing had happened just a few houses down. Jenny had seen from the porch. He had been headed home, and he had lifted up an arm to give her a wave, and then this big lumber supply truck had backed out of a neighbor's driveway, rolling fast down into the street, right into Leo. Jenny had seen him go flying across the road like he weighed nothing, like he was a toy, and she had stayed where she was on the porch swing, rocking back and forth, saying to herself, "That didn't happen. I'm sure that didn't happen."

Jenny turned off the sink and squeezed the socks, one in each fist. On the flight, she would wear a long cotton dress that went all the way down to her feet. When she got off the plane, Leo would be waiting for her. "Let's take the train," he would say. "I'll show you where I've been staying."

By the time Jenny had gotten off the porch and begun running, the truck driver was already kneeling in the road. Leo was unconscious, with one leg twisted around backwards like it didn't belong to his body anymore. The truck driver was crying, Jenny saw that when she got close. He was holding his cell phone in his hand and looking up at her, shaking his head back and forth. "Do something!" Jenny yelled at him, but he had already called for help.

She wondered how many outfits she would need. Would she stay in Leo's smoky little apartment forever, listening to the trains go by in the night? Or would she pack up her things and go out for one last dinner, wear a tight black dress, order a steak and let its juice stain her lips pink, put her hand on Leo's knee under the table and tell him how much she would miss him when she was back home?

The truck driver had come with Jenny to the emergency room. He sat next to her and looked down at the floor. "You know," he told her, "my brother works in an emergency room up in New Hampshire. You wouldn't believe some of the stuff he's seen." She didn't say anything. She was trying not to throw up. "He said one time an old lady got brought in, all alone, for pneumonia. Her throat was dark red and inflamed so my brother, he brought her up some chocolate chip ice cream and when she was eating it, she choked on a chip and died." He looked over at Jenny. "Sorry," he said, "I don't know why I told you that."

Jenny had taken off Leo's socks in the funeral home, peeled them off slow like he had come home from work and she was rubbing the ache from his sweaty feet. The socks were stiff with blood. The tops of Leo's feet had been soft on her fingers, the skin pale and still tender. He had always worn sneakers, kept his feet out of the sun. Jenny wanted to take a pink toenail then, to tug it from his toe and pocket it. Instead, she took the socks and held them in her fists until the dried blood softened enough to stain her palms.

LOST BOYS OF CREATION

HER NAME WAS LIBERTY, but people called her
Libby. She had been called Libby since before she
could remember, although she hated it, although its fat
syllables reminded her of sleep-swollen lips, of the sinew
she could see stretched taut and white from her gums
when she tugged on her lower lip.

Her grandfather had always had thick, rubbery lips.
She could remember him holding her on his lap, hands
clenched beneath her armpits, kissing the top of her head.
"Libby," he would say, "my Libby's getting big," the syllables dropping heavy into her lap, her mother smiling her
encouragement from across the room. "My sweet Libby."

She had hated visiting her grandfather, but he had
traveled for work and sent her the loveliest gifts. From
Moscow, a wooden paddle painted blue and yellow with
chickens that bobbed and pecked at the ground, their
necks tied to a weighted string. In Varanasi he had gotten
her a little pen drawing of the Ganges, done by a riverside

artist on a piece of thick yellow paper. He'd come back from Texas with a spiraling snail fossil that he claimed to have found himself. His best present, though—the one she brought with her to college and then to New York—was from the gift shop at the Louvre, a big glossy book explaining how some of the museum's most famous paintings had been restored to their former glory. Libby loved it, loved the pictures of restoration, of artists working like surgeons to bring the paintings back to life.

Libby had moved to New York after college mostly to be closer to the big paintings, to the masterpieces that she had seen online and in books. She had a job now at the Metropolitan Museum of Art, serving fifteen-dollar cocktails at the Rooftop Garden Bar, listening to museum patrons get drunk and throw around words like *process* and *technique* and *conceptually speaking*.

Some days she'd get to the museum before her shift, sit and look at the paintings, sketch them, imagine she was one of the New York art students who came here every day for class.

She met Jonah at the museum, in front of Gauguin's The Siesta, Libby sitting cross-legged on the floor and studying one of the women in the painting. She had her back to Libby, relaxed, like she'd never known she was being watched.

"Wish she'd turn around," Jonah had said without looking away from the painting, so that Libby had to jerk her head up and look around for someone else before she determined he was talking to her. "Bit voyeuristic, isn't it?" he said.

She had to clear her throat several times and swallow, because her mouth had gone dry in the silence. "Yes," she said finally. "Well, Gauguin was a bit of an ass."

"A talented ass, wasn't he? I'm Jonah, by the way," he said and sat down on the floor beside her, leaning over to see into her sketchbook. She shifted her knees and tried to angle the pages away from him. She had been sketching the woman, adding little faces peering out of the wrinkles in her shirt. They were tired, young faces, skin melting into the fabric and the skin of her back.

"What are those?" asked Jonah. He had seen, despite her best efforts.

"Just a little doodle," she said, and closed the book.

A week later, Jonah showed up at the bar. "I just realized I never caught your name," he explained, and ordered an alcoholic tea drink called "The Good Enough." He was underdressed for the bar and young. He laughed when Libby asked to check his ID. "Haven't been carded since I was sixteen," he said, fishing around in a beat-up leather wallet.

When she brought him the drink, he took one sip and insisted she try it. "I think you'd like it," he said, as though he knew anything at all about what she liked.

"I'm on the clock." She gave him a quick smile.

"When do you get out of here?" he asked. "I'll save you some."

He did save her some, though by the time her shift had ended the ice had melted into the lukewarm drink. "Do you like it?" he asked when she took a sip.

She lied and said yes.

"We could go somewhere else, maybe get something else to drink," he said.

Libby nodded. "Sure," she said, though she wasn't sure why she agreed. There was something about him that made her so aware of her own loneliness.

She told him she wasn't in the mood for a bar, so they went for coffee. It felt like a very New York thing to be doing, getting coffee so late at night, like time and sleep weren't even on their minds. She ordered the darkest roast.

"So," he wanted to know, "are you an artist? I know you like Gauguin."

"He's all right," Libby said. "It's really just that one painting I like."

"What is it about that painting?"

"I don't know." He was asking for a lot of information. She took a sip of her coffee. "What do you do?"

"Oh," he said, "what do I do? A little of everything, really. I'm still in school part time if you can believe it. Taking a couple acting classes, but I think I'll get my degree in physics or business. Sometimes I think I'll just leave, though, you know? Pack it all up and travel around, write some poetry. I have a lot of passions, really."

"Physics," she said. "Why physics?"

"Oh I love the left and the right brain equally," he told her.

Libby didn't know what to say. She took another sip of coffee. She could feel its heat going down her throat, into her stomach. Outside, it was getting dark. The yellow light of the coffee shop had her feeling like an animal in a pet shop display. She kept trying to see out into the street but there was too much light on her, and her own reflection came back to her in the gloss of the window.

"So," Jonah said, "you never told me about being an artist."

"I'm not," she said, then wished she could take it back, say something more vague, less definitive. After all, some days she did consider herself an artist. "I went to school for art conservation."

"Art conservation?"

"Yeah," she said. "I'm applying for this internship at the MoMA actually, but it's pretty competitive so I don't know that I'll get it."

"The MoMA," he said. "Okay, no big deal, the MoMA." He laughed. "So what does an art conservationist do exactly?"

Libby looked down at her hands, the skin cracked and old. Her legs felt jittery from drinking coffee on an empty stomach. "They take care of paintings," she said. She wished she could tell him about her grandfather's rubbery lips, about the wooden chickens with the bobbing necks.

He began to text her more and more often. "Hey Liberty, are you free? (I love a good pun.)" he messaged.

She was turned down for the MoMA internship. She put the letter in the back of her sketchbook, pressed between the cover and the blank pages. She went out on more dates with Jonah. He told her, "Forget that conservationist bullshit. Be a real artist."

She asked him what a real artist was.

He shrugged. "You know."

Jonah lived in an expensive three-bedroom apartment in Brooklyn: big windows, exposed brick, a decorative fireplace in the living room. In the kitchen, one of his roommates had drawn on the walls in green and black Sharpie: "Beware the preachers, beware the knowers." ("Bukowski," Jonah said. "You know him?") Next to the words were twisting figures of nude men, their legs turning into the trunks and roots of trees. Their eyes were big, shaky circles, round and round and round, tired and sunken. Between their legs, the roommate had drawn exaggerated, erect penises. At first, Libby had thought the drawings were just a crude, boyish joke, but both Jonah and his roommate took them very seriously. "The Lost Boys of Creation," they called them, and did not bother to explain to Libby what exactly that meant.

She spent more and more time with him, even stayed over sometimes. When he came down with the flu, she stayed a whole week, bringing him cold washcloths and cups of broth. She was working on an application for a new fellowship at the American Folk Art Museum, and she spent her nights holding her laptop in Jonah's living room, looking into the empty fireplace, listening to his hurried steps to the bathroom.

Libby switched her shifts at work to take care of him. "Who will make the cocktails?" he asked her, his face gray. She didn't answer, just wiped away his sweat and smoothed his damp tendrils of hair. His lips were fever-cracked, with a whitish film that gathered at the corners of his mouth. He had fever dreams about The Lost Boys of Creation. "Just let them fucking take me," he said at one point, tossing and turning in bed. He rolled over and began to caress his pillow. Libby ignored him. She told him about her grandfather's gifts, about the wooden chickens and the little drawing on the yellow paper. When he began to turn the corner, she made him bits of buttered toast with his broth, gave him warm baths, brought him steaming tea, changed the sheets when his fever finally broke. She watched his eyes clear up and the pink come back into his cheeks. She drew a picture of him as he had looked when he was sickest, with his eyes glazed over and his fingers hanging all the way over the edge of the bed, elongated, stretching down to the floor.

When Jonah was healthy enough to eat again, she made linguini, and they ate it for lunch at the kitchen table. The Lost Boys of Creation looked out at them from the walls. "Beware the preachers," they said. Libby tried not to look at their erections.

"Listen," Jonah said, "I really want to thank you for taking care of me like that."

Libby smiled at him, her mouth full.

"But Liberty, I don't want there to be any misunderstanding."

She swallowed her food. "What do you mean?"

"I just mean I think you might be mistaken about what this is."

She shook her head. "What *what* is?"

He cleared his throat. "Us," he said, gesturing at her.

She set her fork down on the edge of her plate.

"I mean," said Jonah, "I think you're great and all—I really do. I just, well I don't want you here all the time, you know?"

"I changed your sheets," Libby said. "I listened to you fucking vomit."

"I know, I know. Thank you," said Jonah. "It's just, I find it all a bit silly. The whole concept of ownership."

"Ownership?"

"You know, monogamy," he said.

Libby nodded. She looked around the dingy kitchen. She didn't even like this guy, didn't want to be sitting in his kitchen. And yet, the thought of getting on the subway, her legs sweating against the orange plastic of the seat, of emerging into the sunshine, of making the short walk to her apartment—it all seemed unbearable. She stayed glued to her seat. "Beware the knowers," the walls told her.

"I mean, sure, one day I'd like to be married, but not now, not while I'm out here, living my life."

Libby looked at him while he talked, imagined how he might look if she dismantled him and then put him back together, a little skin here, a freckle there.

"Is there someone else?" she asked. It felt like a very stupid question.

"Not someone per se," Jonah explained.

She imagined the not-someone to be very tall and willowy, with a hip, short haircut, maybe a nose ring, a job at a bookshop. Maybe she was a real artist. Maybe she did more than piece together what had already been made. Maybe, when she was asked, she said flat out, "Yes, I am an artist," and after a few drinks she would uncap her Sharpie and draw her own figure on the wall, and she would give it big, beautiful nipples that Jonah and his roommates would find vaguely political.

"I just wanted to make sure we were on the same page," Jonah was saying.

Libby remembered his gray face and his split lips.

She got up to go. "You looked fallow," she said, although she wasn't sure if she meant *fallow* or *foul*.

She left the apartment, let the door swing shut behind her. She rode the subway downtown and stopped for a cup of coffee. She ordered the dark roast and drank it too fast, burnt her tongue. It was afternoon, and she could see out into the street. A woman walked past wearing a sunhat with a ribbon tied around the brim. She was holding a bouquet of yellow roses, using both arms to cradle them like a child. Libby ordered a second cup of coffee. She could feel the jitters starting up in her feet.

She kept biting down hard on her burnt, fuzzy-feeling tongue.

She got up and left the coffee shop, headed for the Met. It was cool inside and full of small sounds: shoes clicking, paper rustling, little coughs and whispers. Libby took the elevator up to the Gauguin exhibit and sat down in front of *The Siesta* to look at the women again, at their colorful clothes in the afternoon light. Libby's favorite woman was propped up on her forearms, staring at something out past the edge of the canvas. Her dress was orange, the color of a ripe cantaloupe. Libby could imagine mixing the color, touching up little corners of the dress that had gone dull with age. She traced a deep green shadow to the back of the painting where another woman sat with her back to the viewer. She was smaller and less graceful, her knees coming up on either side of her like a frog's. Libby wondered if she was lonely looking down at all that grass and dirt. She wondered if she could hear the voices of the other women in the painting, if she could hear out into the gallery, hear a man whisper to his friends about the way the painting glorified the privacy of the everyday. "Privacy," he said, "that's hard to come by nowadays."

Libby turned to look at the man. He looked a bit like Jonah—the same reddish beard and mustache, the same hands-in-his-pockets stance. The good enough, Libby thought, and smiled. She wasn't sad, exactly, she just felt like one of those wooden chickens, getting her neck tugged down by the same string as everybody else.

CARLO'S FISH

THE SUMMER BEFORE I LOST CARLO, I started having this dream that my skin was made of glass. There were nights when I would wake up with my shirt pulled up past my nipples and I would catch my breath, thinking a stranger was in the room with me, touching me. "You're going to break me," I wanted to tell them. "You have to be careful."

I don't mean that Carlo died. I mean that I killed his fish. I killed his fish and he left me. He'd had those fish for almost two years. "Longer than you've been around," he said, which wasn't true. I'd been with him when he bought the tank and the blue pebbles to spread on the bottom. We had only just started seeing each other. "I don't get it," I had said. "Why fish?"

Carlo said he liked fish because they were clean. He said it was nice watching them swim, relaxing how easy their lives were, how they lived in silence. He liked putting his hands into the tank and making little waves and whirl-pools, currents that carried the fish any whichway. "Look at them go," he would say. "This feels like a hurricane to them, I bet."

I'd met Carlo at the summer carnival. He'd been working the Ferris wheel, which he said was a pretty big deal, since it had the widest range of clientele. Kids, old people, teen-agers, you name it. Lots of people to please.

He'd given me a free ride, and the funny thing is that when I was in my little cart, all the way at the top of the Ferris wheel—that was probably when I loved him most. Even though I didn't know him, even though all I could see of him was the top of his head getting smaller and closer and smaller again.

Another funny thing was that after the rides had shut down for the night, Carlo took me on a walk through the fairgrounds and we saw one of those old carnival games, a kiddy pool full of rubber ducks and a shelf of fish in Ziploc bags that you could win as prizes. Carlo showed me the fish, smiling. "Aren't they something?"

"Really something," I'd said, like it wasn't the saddest thing I'd ever seen.

Carlo said he didn't remember meeting me at the carni-val. He didn't remember the kiddy pools or the fish in the plastic bags. "I never would've given anyone a free ride," he said. "It was against policy."

According to him, we met at the hospital, where I was working in the call center. When I picked up the phone, I had to say, "Hello, how can I help you?" like I was taking an order at a drive-thru. These days most hospitals have an automated recording that directs patients to different departments. *Press 1 for triage, press 2 for oncology.*

I was working the overnight shift when Carlo called. This is the part we both remember.

"Hello, how can I help you?" I said.

There was no response, just loud gasps of breath.

"How can I help you?" I repeated, pressing the receiver closer to my ear. More breathing. "Are you having an asthma attack?" When there was still no response, I started to get annoyed. "Well, why didn't you call 911?" The breathing became more urgent. It sounded like the person on the other end had begun to bang their hand on the counter. "Okay," I said, "okay, I'm sending someone over. Would you like to stay on the phone with me?" The person banged their hand more on the counter. I matched the phone number to an address and switched lines to order an ambulance. Then I switched back. "I'm still here," I said. "It's going to be okay." I wondered if it really would be okay. I wondered if I was going to hear this person die, alone in their home, imagined discovering them days later, body spotted with black rot.

They brought him in and gave him a steroid to get his breathing back on track. Then, when that was over, he came and found me in the lobby.

"I'd like to buy you a drink," he said. "You saved my life."

His face was still gray and damp with sweat. I would've said no, only at the last second I recognized him from the Ferris wheel. I swear that really happened. All of it—the Ferris wheel, the ducks, the bags of fish. I had him bend over right there in the hospital so I could take a look at the top of his head and it was Carlo, it really was, coming into focus as I rode the wheel back down.

On our date, I told Carlo that I'd gotten the job in the call center because I loved helping people. "Yes," I said, "I think this is what I was meant to do."

It was a lie. I didn't believe I was meant to do anything at all, necessarily, let alone work the overnight shift at the call center. I wanted Carlo to think I was a good person. I kept watching him, imagining his lips opening and closing, trying to draw air, eyes bulging. I imagined his fist banging on the counter and how my voice must have sounded over the phone. *Hello, how can I help you?*

I ordered a cranberry juice and Carlo ordered a glass of red wine. "They look the same," he said, which wasn't true. "So, what's your family like?" he wanted to know.

I told him that my mother was an opera singer in New York and that my father bred Clydesdales for Anheuser-Busch in New Hampshire.

"You're kidding," he said.

"No." I was, but I didn't tell him that. My mother

worked customer service at State Farm and my father taught third grade at the local elementary school. I had a brother too, but he was dead.

My brother dying wasn't a recent thing. It had happened when I was four and he was six. He had fallen in the river and been washed away.

When, much later, I told Carlo the truth about my family, he hugged me. "And what was that like?" he asked after I mentioned the river, the slippery rocks, the way my brother's hair had swirled in the water when we found him downstream.

"What was it like?"

He nodded and touched my arm. I jerked away. His fingers felt too strong, like they'd pull the skin right off my body.

Later, we listened to old opera recordings, and I closed my eyes and pretended the voice was my mother. My mother the opera singer. My mother from New York.

Sometimes, I thought about how my parents would have sounded on the phone if they had called in to the hospital. *"Hello, how can I help you?"*

"Our son, he's hit his head on the rocks! I don't know if he's breathing!"

"He's hit his head on the rocks?"

"Yes, in the river!"

"Okay, can you give us an address? We'll send someone right over."

And the bright sunlight, the wet hair. The daughter screaming in the background. Bloated boy, crying mother. *"Hello, how can I help you?"*

When Carlo came home and saw his dead fish, he got very quiet. He was quiet all night, all morning. By afternoon he was on the train to Boston. He took a suitcase with him. "Probably won't be back," he said when he left.

"Probably won't be back."

Once, we'd gone to the aquarium and seen fish with see-through skin. There had been a feeding demonstration where we could watch the fish digest their food, see it moving through their bodies in little black clumps. That was how my skin felt, too. Like everyone could see things moving around in my body, all my bitter clumps of phlegm and bile.

Carlo wanted to hold my hand the whole way home from the aquarium. It was a three-hour bus ride from Boston. I could feel the sweat from his palms leaking moisture into my pores, leaving salt crusted on the raised bits of my skin. "We can't hold hands right now," I told him and pressed my palms up against the cold of the window for some relief.

"Why?"

"We just can't."

I thought he might bruise me if he touched me. I thought my clothes might leave marks up against my skin. "I need to take my clothes off," I said. "I think I need to take them off very soon."

Carlo nuzzled up against my neck. His nose was cold and wet like a cat's.

"Not like that."

I worried that Carlo could read my thoughts through the heat of my skin. I wondered if he knew that in high school I'd been invited to a pool party and had so much raspberry sorbet and pink champagne that I'd thrown up in the water and the vomit had spread around me like a rosy halo. Or that I'd been to a wedding once, on a boat, and the couple had put out little jars of orange goldfish as centerpieces, and the goldfish had all gone belly-up from the rocking of the boat.

There were some things that Carlo didn't know about me, that he never knew about me.

One day, Carlo went out and bought a big metal pot. "I'm making stew," he told me, and began to slice up some potatoes.

"I don't like stew," I told him.

"You'll like this one," he said, smiling.

I thought about it all day. *"You'll like this one."* When he finally served me a bowl, watched me take the first bite, chew the meat, swallow—that was when I knew. He could see through me. Through my pale, clear spots. He wanted to feed me the stew and watch how it went through my body, how my organs clenched and swallowed.

I could not eat in front of him. I could not eat at all.

I waited for him to go to work the next morning. He would be gone for the weekend at a conference down in Boston. *Thank god.* I would be able to eat. He kissed me on the shoulder before he went, left behind a mouth-shaped bruise.

When he was gone, when I was sure he couldn't see me, I went into the kitchen and poured myself a glass of water. Several glasses of water. The insides of my throat had dried in the night.

Carlo claimed this next part was on purpose, but I swear that it wasn't.

I went into his study, where the fish were, and I shook little flakes of food onto the surface of the water. The fish came swimming up to the surface to eat. I leaned closer. I could see their little mouths opening and closing around the flakes, lips pursed like they were gasping for air. Did they swallow? I leaned closer. I shook more food into the water, then more and more. Pretty soon, the whole container was gone. The flakes covered the top of the tank like algae.

The next morning, the fish were belly up. "Little fish," I said. "Little fish." They bobbed up and down in the dirty water but didn't respond. When I leaned in, I thought I could see their sides pulsing, a heartbeat in their stomachs. I was wrong, of course.

I brought the tank into the bedroom, put my hands into the water, and scooped out a fish. I laid it down on the pillow. Cold water stained the pillowcase. I reached for the next one, for the next one. I wanted them to cover the pillow, wanted to lie back and wear them as a crown. I wanted to swallow them whole. I wanted Carlo to watch them slide down.

I can't explain what happened, can't tell you why I did what I did. I couldn't explain it to him either when he came home to find me sleeping with the fish dried up around my face. "What have you done?" He screamed, and looked at me like I was a stranger.

If a fish dries out enough, its skin turns to paper and its skeleton comes through.

I don't think Carlo knew that.

SPIDER BITE

J AY WAS BITTEN BY A BLACK WIDOW only two
weeks after he came back from the war. He had two tiny
red pinpricks in the crook of his knee that swelled and
burned, made him queasy and short of breath. His wife
Sherri crushed the spider under her heel and put it into a
jam jar so they could show the doctor the round marble
of its body, the red hourglass on its back.

Jay had to stay inside after that, with his leg elevated to
keep the swelling down. Sherri stayed by him, washing the
bite with soap and water, icing it numb four times a day,
rubbing Neosporin on the pinpricks with the very tip of
her finger, angled just right so that her fingernail wouldn't
snag on the wound.

"At least you didn't lose your leg," she kept saying. "We
can be thankful for that."

It was spring, and she kept the windows open. "For Jay," she said. So he could smell the grass and hear the birds. Sometimes she sat by him and pointed out the window. She knew all the types of birds, their colors and their songs. "Jay," she would say, touching his arm or the base of his elevated thigh, "look how red that cardinal is. I think that's the reddest I've ever seen." She even kept the window open when it rained, just a crack, so Jay could smell the mud pooling outside beneath the window and in the old rutted driveway.

Once, before he had enlisted, he and Sherri had seen a hawk dive into a meadow and come up with a mouse in its beak. "Now there's a bird," he'd said, and she had craned her neck to watch it fly away.

These days Sherri worked the breakfast shift at a diner in town, so Jay had the mornings to himself. He liked the shades down when he was alone, the house full of gray, filtered light. She usually left him with two slices of bread and a few pieces of salami. He'd take the salami in his hand, lay it against his palm for a long time, roll it against the veins in his wrist, and let it cool his blood. When he peeled it off it would be warm and sticky, and he would tear it into bits to remind himself it was salami—just a slice of salami on bread, with no flesh that might shudder or gasp for breath or grip at his fingers as he ate.

Before he'd gotten the spider bite, Sherri had been planning a big dinner party, splurging on fancy ketchup and a pineapple, asking if it would be in poor taste to invite Jeanine, if that would be rubbing in her face how Jay had made it back in one piece and Bobby had not.

After the bite, she told Jay they had all that pineapple and ketchup anyway, and would it be okay if she still had the party—she understood if it wouldn't be. He said sure, go ahead, because he could see how much it meant to her. Earlier in the day she had heard two goldfinches singing to each other and had run downstairs, out of breath, to point them out. "The females weave their nests so tight they can fill up with water," she had told him. She'd always loved seeing birds, but when Jay was gone she had read up on them, pages and pages of facts on all her sleepless nights. On their wedding day, Jay had seen six goldfinches on his way into the church. Sherri said it was a good omen. She liked to tell Jay every time she saw one now, even if Jay wasn't there to see it too. Jay agreed to the dinner party because he didn't care much about goldfinches anymore and because sometimes, in his worst moments, he couldn't even remember the details of their wedding, the specific way that Sherri had looked or the words either of them had said. He didn't care about those things anymore, but he wanted to.

The day of the party was overcast. Sherri set up card tables on either end of the dining room table and covered them with paper tablecloths. There was potato salad and macaroni with sliced hotdogs and green Jell-O with chunks of floating pineapple. Jay was propped up in one corner, his leg elevated away from the table, a scarf tied around it to cover the wound.

Jeanine sat across from him and stared at his leg. "Do you still have it?" she asked. "The spider?"

"Sure," Jay said. "Sherri stomped on it pretty good, though."

Sherri shot him a look from across the table. Jay picked up a hardboiled egg, cupped it with both hands, ignoring her.

"Can I see it?" Jeanine wanted to know.

"Sure," Jay said. "You'll have to go get it. It's on the nightstand in the bedroom. Down at the end of that hallway."

Sherri shot him another look. "Maybe after we eat," she said, but Jeanine was already headed down the hallway.

She came back with the jam jar, holding it up to the light from the window, moving it around so that the spider slid and bumped against the glass. Its legs were askew, bent sideways by the weight of Sherri's foot.

"She's little," Jeanine said, unscrewing the lid and tipping the body out into her hand. Jay could see where the head had been split open. He began to peel apart his hardboiled egg. He could smell it coming out of the shell. The inner membrane of the eggshell pieces puckered and crinkled. He had been the one to find Bobby's body, had seen the layers of his skin beginning to blister and separate. He wondered how much Jeanine—or anyone at the table—knew about a body decomposing.

Jeanine put the spider on the table and began touching each of its legs, following their crooked lines with the very tip of her finger. Everyone at the table was watching her. Only Jay was eating, pulling the white from the yolk with his front teeth.

"Maybe we should put that away," Sherri said from her end of the table. "It turns my stomach a bit." She giggled. Jeanine scooped the spider into the palm of her hand, but made no move to put it back in the jar.

Jay shifted in his seat to grab another egg and the scarf came loose and slid down his leg. His wound was round and black, stretched taut over the creases where his knee might've bent.

"Look!" Sherri said. "An oriole. There's an oriole at the feeder. They're very rare."

No one turned to look.

"I wish to god it was Bobby who'd gotten that bite," Jeanine said, very quietly, pushing the tiny legs into line. She was trying to bend them, to prop the spider up so it would look alive, like it might crawl across the table at any moment, crushed head and all.

Who Will Keep You
Safe Tonight

In five years, Lane thought, she would not even remember the way she felt now. She pushed her sunglasses onto the top of her head and squinted out at the road, at the big orange sun winking in front of the house, obliterating a section of the roof, a room or two of the upstairs.

"Okay," she said. "Okay." And she willed herself to go inside.

The house was full of the thick, salty smell of ham. "Honey glazed," her mom said. Her hair was pulled back into a tight knot at the nape of her neck. There was gray now, even some white. She was stirring a pot of applesauce on the stove, tapping the cinnamon jar, shaking more in. "Come over here," she said, "so I can see you."

Lane moved closer to the stove. The last rays of light came slanting in through the window and blinded her.

She blinked and looked down. She could feel her mom's eyes on her, moving around, taking her in. Her clothes were scrubbed clean, stiff and tight against her skin. She reached her thumbs through her belt loops and tugged her pants up. "Well," she said, "here I am."

Lane heard her dad cough upstairs. "Hello?" he called out.

"I'm here." She heard his footsteps on the stairs.

"Lane?"

"Yes."

"It's been a while," he said, coming into the kitchen. Lane stood still, letting him look her over. It had been almost three years since she had been in this kitchen.

Her dad sniffed the air. "Smells good," he said. "Your mom's been cooking all day."

Lane nodded. Three years since she had told them they could go to hell for all she cared, actually said those words.

"Maybe you could help your mom out," Lane's dad said. "Set the table."

"Sure." She opened up the silverware drawer, pulled out forks, knives, spoons. "Anyone else going to be home?"

"Your brothers are at work," her mom said.

"Man, those boys can work," said her dad.

"Always working," her mom said.

"Jack's got a job up at the hardware store now," her dad said, "mixing the paint colors."

"Among other things," said her mom.

"Anyway," said her dad, "just us three tonight. Your

sister's at her boyfriend's house, and afterwards she's all tied up babysitting."

"She's getting very mature," said her mom.

"I know," said Lane, "I've seen her."

"You've seen her?"

"Yes," said Lane. "She didn't tell you we stayed in touch?"

"Maybe she—"

"She must've and it just slipped our minds," her dad said, clearing his throat.

Lane nodded. She pulled napkins from the drawer and grabbed the salt and pepper shakers by their tops, clinking them together into one fist. The dining room was cool and dark, with green walls and cream-colored curtains pulled closed.

When the table was set and the food was served, they held hands and Lane's dad said grace. "Amen," Lane said when he had finished, the word hollow and sticky in her throat.

"So," Lane's mom said, dragging a bite of ham through her applesauce and studiously not looking up, "how's Kit? Do you hear from her?"

"She's fine," Lane said.

"Still a vegan?" her dad asked.

"She wasn't a vegan. She was gluten free."

"Just about all that girl ate was sweet potatoes," her dad said. He shook his head, working on slicing the rind from the edge of his ham.

Kit ate much more than sweet potatoes. The first time they had breakfast together, she had cooked up six fried eggs and four links of turkey sausage, split them between two large bowls of greens, sprinkled the whole thing over with salt, pepper, and cayenne, sliced up a side dish of apples slathered over with peanut butter, brewed a six-cup pot of coffee, brought out a whole pitcher of milk— and all that for just the two of them. Lane had never eaten so much in her life. "Breakfast is a power meal," Kit had explained, splitting the yolks of her eggs open so they ran down into the greens.

Lane ate her entire breakfast so as not to disappoint. Kit, it turned out, had a rigid but unspoken daily routine that Lane found herself drawn into without quite realizing what was happening. Kit woke every morning at 6:30 and the first thing she did was pull on her work boots, so by the time she had clomped her way down the stairs, Lane was awake too. When Lane came downstairs, Kit already had the sausage crackling in its pan. After breakfast, Lane headed out to work at a bakery up in town and Kit took the dogs for a run, two by two, so that by the time she had finished she had run eight times as much as any one dog. She ate a protein bar for lunch, gulped down water, and got ready for an afternoon of training exercises with the dogs and entertaining clients. Lane came home sometime in the middle of all this, tired and sweaty and smelling like bread, and Kit would drag her out to help with the dogs. For dinner, they ate salad with protein—beans or fish, occasionally chicken. Then they read or paid bills for an hour, checked on the dogs, and went to bed at sundown. "The body's natural rhythms," Kit explained. "You can't beat 'em."

Lane had met Kit through a Craigslist ad for a bedroom in a house by a lake, big backyard, five hundred a month. The lease was June through August with the option to renew in September. Must be comfortable with dogs.

Kit, it turned out, was a dog trainer. She had sixteen pit bull terriers penned in the backyard. She was training them to be guard dogs, attack dogs. "They won't hurt you," she said when she introduced them. "Not with me here anyway. Here, give Maisie a biscuit. I think she likes you."

Maisie had been eyeing Lane from a few feet away, a low growl building in her throat. She was a dull orange, short and stocky with a big, broad skull and a divot smack in the middle of her forehead. She looked a little like Kit. Muscle balled and knotted across Maisie's chest. Her lips drooped at the edges, revealing black gums and the glint of her incisors. Lane held the biscuit out in the flat of her palm and prayed for Maisie to like her.

"She's just figuring you out," Kit said. "She's a real sweetheart once she gets to know you."

"Oh, I can see that." Maisie's rubbery lips rode up over her teeth and she snapped the biscuit from Lane's hand.

"Now what I teach them is not to be vicious," Kit said. "It's to be loyal. Real loyal. These dogs would take a bullet for me." She chuckled. "Not that they'd have to. They know to go straight for a gunman's jugular. Eliminate the threat entirely."

Lane nodded. "Smart."

Lane's room was already partially furnished when she moved in. There was a full-sized bed, a little wooden dresser, and a framed painting hanging on the wall above her bed. The painting was from the Battle of the Somme, of five soldiers lined up in a trench with their gas masks on. Lane wasn't sure if Kit had put it there on purpose or not, so she left it up to be safe. She didn't have much in the way of décor anyway. Just a framed photograph of herself, her sister, and her brothers all lined up in matching white T-shirts and a little wooden crucifix she'd gotten for her eleventh birthday, which she hung.

"Minimalist," Kit said when she saw Lane's bedroom. "I like it."

"My god, what is that painting?" Lane's mom said when she visited.

"Well, it's only 'til August," Lane's dad said. "Then you can come right back home."

Lane was the oldest of five children. She had grown up changing diapers, washing diapers, giving baths in the sink, grinding up wet baby food in the food processor. She knew just how to hold a baby's head when the skull was still soft and new. She knew all about babies.

Dogs, it turned out, were not so different from babies. The trick was to tire them out. At first, Lane stood only just inside the pen, back pressed up against the chain-link fence, and tossed bits of kindling for them to chase down and slobber over. They were strong, energetic dogs and it took a while to get them tired out, but when she did, they were docile, almost cuddly, lying down with their chins on top of their paws.

Maisie warmed up to Lane first. She was not so bad after all—she was actually a bit of a runt and seemed to have trouble fitting in. She had her food stolen from her by some of the other dogs, and when Lane came to play fetch, Maisie was always careful to hang back and wait for her turn. She had a bald, gray scar on her back, just above her tail, that she had a self-conscious habit of licking and biting. When she slept, her forehead wrinkled up into worry lines. She seemed to sense in Lane something that comforted her, perhaps Lane's own fear, her own coiled leg muscles and the way she never opened the gate more than a crack, just barely enough for her to slip inside.

Maisie began napping on her foot while the other dogs played catch, chin resting on the steel toe of Lane's boot. She let her scratch between her ears, down her spine, even the tender area around her scar. She let her talk to her too. "Hi baby, aren't you cute?" and "Look how strong you're getting!" and "Look at us now, Maisie girl. What're we gonna do now?" and other things, too, that Lane didn't say, exactly, but that she felt Maisie knew. Things about her family and how she knew she was disappointing them, or at least had them worried she might disappoint them. How she'd never learned to do anything in this world but mother a baby, and maybe that was not what she wanted to do. Even if she loved her baby siblings, even if she didn't regret that part of her life one bit.

Kit was pleased with Lane's progress with the dogs, Maisie in particular. "Now the trick is not really to make her like you," Kit counseled. "That can be a problem. What you want is respect."

She taught her some of the basic commands, which were all in German, and how to pitch her voice when she said them. "Police dog tactic," she explained. She showed Lane how to keep her grip on a leash, how to stand with her feet spread wide apart and planted firmly on the ground. During training sessions, she had to stand with the dog's leash in her hand, waiting for a hired stranger to jump out from behind a tree or a bush, bundled up in an attack suit. The goal was to get the dog as riled up as possible, tensed and snarling, ropes of drool, flashing teeth, ready to leap at the intruder's throat. Lane would hold the leash very tightly with both hands. Then Kit would yell, "*Lass es!*" ("Leave it!"), and the dog would go soft, groveling in the dirt at Lane's feet.

They performed these demonstrations for potential buyers to show them how safe they could be with Maisie or Chuck or Growler. "This ain't some fireside lapdog," Kit liked to say. "What you're getting is a personal protection dog. An attack dog. Someone to keep you safe at night. This here is a dog who will respect you, who will follow your every order—sit, stay, and sic."

•

They got some pretty odd customers, being in the business of selling attack dogs. In June, just after Lane moved in, someone showed up asking if pit bulls made good meat, should an emergency arise. In July, a man wanted to know if it was true pit bulls ate babies. Others asked sly questions about tooth size and ferocity, if they could fight anything besides a human—rats, say—and Kit would send them away without another word. Nothing upset her worse than blood sports.

In August, a couple showed up wanting to know if a pit bull could last for long periods of time in a limited space, possibly without sun—a bunker, say—and only if necessary, of course. They were an older couple, both with thick, matted white hair tied up with ribbon into loose, random clumps. Crazy, Lane thought. Wild-eyed conspiracy theorists. She snuck looks at Kit throughout their visit as though to say, "My god, let's get them out of here," but Kit ignored her and instead spoke seriously with the couple, discussing minimum bunker square footage and exercise regimes that could be executed in confinement.

When the couple left, Lane rolled her eyes. "What was that about?"

Kit was quiet.

"I mean, never mind how bad that kind of confinement is for a dog—think what it does to a human." She glanced at Kit. "If the apocalypse comes, leave me to die, that's what I always say. You won't catch me feasting on baby flesh to survive."

"Survival isn't a joke, Lane."

Lane laughed but wished she hadn't. "What? Do you have a bunker hidden underground somewhere?"

"I sure do," Kit said.

The iron door was set in the side of a hill, nearly hidden by pines. That was as far as Kit would take her. "You aren't ready. I won't let you in just to have a laugh."

Lane apologized again and again. "I guess," she said, "I just wasn't raised to take this kind of thing seriously."

The two of them walked down to the lake in silence. Lane kept sneaking glances at Kit. How had she built an entire bunker? Didn't that take all sorts of equipment, all sorts of skill? How much money did she have anyway?

At the edge of the lake, Kit slipped her shoes off, climbed onto a flat, low rock, and dangled her feet into the water, swirling them around to scare off the minnows. Lane slipped her shoes off and found her own rock, dark gray and warm from the sun.

"What did you mean by that?" Kit asked. The anger was gone from her voice. "When you said you weren't raised to take survival seriously?"

"Not survival," Lane said. "The end of the world. I wasn't raised to think that was coming. And if it was, well then, it was next stop: Heaven."

"Really?" Kit asked. "You believe in Heaven?"

"My family does. Heaven, Hell, Father, Son. All that."

"And you?"

"I guess I don't know."

Kit nodded. She was squinting. "Well I think this is all I've got, right here. And I think it's worth protecting." She swung her arm out across the lake, sparkling as the sun went down, up to the house, barking coming down through the pines, little yips and squeals, low growls that built to a crescendo and broke into snarls.

In September, Lane renewed her lease at the house on the lake.

"I was hoping you would," Kit said.

"You were?" Lane asked, and then was giddy all day with a kind of childish excitement.

When she called her parents to let them know, they were quiet on the other end of the line.

"Are you sure about this?" her dad said finally.

"You know you're always welcome here," her mom said. "There's no shame in moving back home."

Lane rolled her eyes. "Put Catherine on the phone," she said. "I wanna talk to her."

Lane's sister was only fourteen. She squealed when she heard Lane still had a place of her own. "So cool," she said. "Maybe I can visit sometime, just me?"

"Of course," Lane said, feeling generous and old. "I'll get wine if you promise not to tell."

Kit was not pleased about having a houseguest. "I don't want you two playing with the dogs," she said. "You're already spoiling Maisie, making her go soft." But the morning before Catherine arrived, Kit went to the store and picked up extra groceries. "Hope she likes her eggs over-easy. That's the only way I make 'em," she grumbled when Lane tried to thank her.

Catherine wouldn't say what she thought of the house. She looked all around with wide eyes at the little house with the curtains pulled shut, the pine tree shadows creeping across the lawn, the rocky path down to the lake, Kit wrangling the dogs behind the tall chain-link fence.

"We're learning about World War I in school," she said when she saw the painting in Lane's room. "*Dulce et decorum est*, right? Did you know mustard gas literally makes you cough up a lung? Like, it comes out in chunks."

Over dinner, Catherine grew bolder. She topped off her own wine glass once, twice, a third time. "Kit," she said, "this salad is amazing. I'm actually thinking about going vegan, but Mom says it's not a good idea because I'm still growing. She says all kinds of things, though. The other day, when she found out about Jackson, she asked me if I was going to marry him someday. Literally marry him. Can you believe that? I'm fourteen! I told her, 'No, Mom, this isn't the sixteenth century.'"

Kit excused herself as soon as she was done eating. "Off to bed," she mumbled. "Goodnight."

"God," Catherine whispered to Lane, "she goes to bed early." She took another sip of wine. "Not that that's a bad thing or anything, just kinda weird. I like her, though, and I can tell you do too."

Lane nodded. "Sure," she said. "She's a good roommate."

"But that's not all," Catherine whispered. "Is it?"

Lane took a sip of wine herself. She could feel her face

going red, and she wanted to explain to Catherine that it was the wine making her flush—nothing else. "I mean, we're friends," Lane said.

Catherine leaned in, eyes wide and serious. "I thought you guys were in love."

Lane laughed. "I think the wine's getting to you."

"I'm not judging," Catherine insisted. "There's nothing wrong with that."

"I know there's nothing wrong with that," Lane snapped. "That's just not the way it is."

And it wasn't the way it was, Lane thought, over and over, replaying her conversation with Catherine in her head. It really wasn't. She didn't think of Kit that way, and never had, not until her sister brought it up. But now Lane couldn't get the thought out of her head. She turned it over and over and felt it growing in the pit of her stomach too, carving out space, making a home. She was angry with Catherine for giving her this feeling, or the idea for this feeling. She was angry watching the dogs growl and snap during training, watching the muscles in Kit's thighs tense as she squatted to the ground, face red and sweaty, screaming in German. She was angry and embarrassed, too, when Kit called out "*Lass es!*" and the dogs fell at her feet, groveling and whining, leashes slack in Lane's fist.

Lane started taking Maisie for evening runs, short at first, as her lungs adjusted to the exercise, then longer as her breathing slowed and the muscles in her calves thickened.

She ran Maisie right down the center of the road. If any traffic came their way, Maisie barked a mile-long warning, bristling, trained and ready to eliminate the threat. Lane had to stand strong with her feet planted to keep her from lunging at vehicles, snapping her teeth at the rubber tires. When no one was around, Lane ran little stretches with her eyes closed, listening to her heartbeat pounding in her eardrums. Maisie ran with her tongue out, catching blackflies and gnats.

Lane would run as far as she could, then walk home, panting. "Maisie," she would ask, "what's the difference between love and admiration?" And "Maisie"— shaking her head now—"what would my mother think?"

The old couple—the ones with the bunker—came back in October and bought Growler.

"These are the end times," the man said. "All the signs are there."

Lane didn't laugh this time or shoot looks at Kit. "What are the signs?" she asked.

"Bad weather patterns," he said. "Video chatting. We were warned of these things."

Later that afternoon, Kit agreed to take Lane into the bunker. Lane went first, climbing down the ladder into the darkness. When her foot hit solid ground, she stepped to the side to make room for Kit. Lane had no sense of the room at all, only of a damp chill that settled over her skin. She shivered, thinking of Growler in his new home.

Kit fumbled in the darkness, banged her elbow on something, swore, and finally managed to switch on the light. Even then, the room was dim, but Lane was shocked by how big it was. Rows and rows of canned food lined the walls. There were five-gallon tanks of water stacked in one corner and heaped bags of dog food in another. Several lawn chairs had been folded and stacked against the back wall along with an antique hospital cot on rusted wheels.

"My parents used to have one of these," Lane said, fiddling with the metal crank at the foot of the cot so that the mattress sat up and then lay back down again. "When any of the younger kids got sick, they got to lie in it, even for meals. I'd crank them up to a seated position and put a tray over their lap, just like in a real hospital. And if they were really sick, they got to say grace with just their hearts and not their words."

Kit wasn't listening. She was across the room, rustling around in the back of one of the shelves.

"Hey," Lane called over to her, "this place is incredible." She tried to put an extra note of sincerity into her voice. An apology for being disrespectful in the first place.

Kit emerged, holding something above her head, a can of Del Monte pear halves with a tab for easy access, like a can of soda. They sat on the cot and dug their fingers deep into the juice, grabbing hold of the slippery fruit, syrup dripping down their wrists. Kit hiked a leg up onto the cot, so her knee rested against Lane's thigh, and Lane hated herself for how she stared down at the place their legs touched, how her heartbeat quickened in her ears, how her hand trembled, just for a moment, long enough for syrup to drip from the half-eaten pear in her hand and into the crook of Kit's knee so that she jumped, moved her leg, and set her foot back down on the floor.

By winter, Lane had fallen so deeply in love that she didn't think twice about it when Kit suggested, over breakfast, that she quit her job at the bakery and dedicate more of her time to helping with the dogs. Kit had been in talks with a breeder recently, and was expecting a shipment of puppies in the spring.

"Absolutely," Lane said, mashing her greens into the runny egg yolk at the bottom of her bowl. "I think that's a great idea."

"Puppies are hard work," Kit warned, "so don't go thinking this'll be easy."

Lane had some savings set aside, but even with Kit buying most of the groceries and cutting the rent in half for Lane's help with the dogs, the money went fast. She monitored her account on her phone, and when the balance sank below seventy dollars, she called home.

"Just to get me through the winter," Lane promised. "Spring is the busy season and I'll be making commission." An assumption—not anything she had ever discussed with Kit, but she said it anyway. "I'll be fine then, I promise. Please," she added.

Lane's parents insisted on visiting for a second time before they would write her the check.

"You can trust me," Lane said. "You don't have to come check on me." She went into the bathroom and looked herself over. She was bigger now and more muscular. Her shirt was muddy and torn from work with the dogs, the armpits darkened with sweat stains.

"Well, we'd like to see you," Lane's dad said.

"And make sure we aren't funding some kind of meth addiction," said her mom.

They drove down the Saturday before Christmas. Lane had spent the morning in her room, rifling through her dresser for her cleanest shirt and a nice pair of black jeans. Then, at the last second, she'd stripped it all off in favor of yesterday's sweaty long johns, ripped jeans, and old sweatshirt. She'd give them a chance to see what her life was really like. Who she was becoming.

"Oh," said Lane's dad when she saw her, "is your washing machine broken?"

Lane took them to see the dogs, introducing them one by one. She called Maisie, who licked her fingers but growled at her parents and refused to get too close. "She's a real sweetheart once she gets to know you," Lane promised.

She handed out bits of cold chicken for her parents to hold in their outstretched palms. They were good sports, crouching in the snow and making kissy noises until Maisie approached with her nose twitching. She was still small, but she had built muscle from her extra runs with Lane. Her legs and chest rippled as she walked. She swallowed the chicken, then went to lie at Lane's feet, permitting her mom to scratch very gently between her ears.

"See?" said Lane. "I told you."

For dinner, her parents offered to take her out. "Your roommate can come too," her dad said. "What's her name again?"

Lane shook her head. "Kit," she said. "And I think we'll eat dinner here."

"You don't want to go out?"

"We kind of have a routine." She was annoyed she had to explain this. "Kit makes salad."

Lane's mom sighed and slapped her hands against her hips. "Salad it is," she said.

Kit didn't talk much over dinner, which wasn't unusual, but with her parents there, Lane felt the silence like a dead weight that settled around her shoulders. She stared across the table at Kit. The way she speared her lettuce with quick, sharp jabs of her fork. The way her eyelids lowered halfway when she swallowed.

"Kit's getting in a shipment of puppies," Lane said.

Her parents smiled.

"Kit's trained four generations of puppies out here."

Lane couldn't stop.

"People think these dogs are vicious, but they're actually just loyal. The first time I met Kit . . ."

On and on she went until Kit got up, cleared her plate, and announced she was headed up to bed.

When Kit was gone, Lane's mom leaned across the table. "I'm sorry," she said, "but you know I can't condone this kind of lifestyle. Why don't you come home and I'll set you up with someone nice. One of the interns from your dad's work. Or whatever happened to Eric from high school?"

"He was a nice boy," Lane's dad confirmed. "Knew how to handle himself around adults."

"What are you talking about?" Lane said. She stood up, brought the dishes to the sink, and began to rinse out the salad bowls. Bits of wet lettuce stuck to her fingers and she flicked them off onto the edge of the sink.

"What your mom is trying to say," Lane's dad said, speaking very slowly like he was having trouble choosing his words, "is that we don't feel entirely comfortable with this living situation. It's ungodly. And frankly, I wouldn't be able to live with myself knowing I was paying for you to live this way."

"Come home," said Lane's mom. "We miss you."

Lane clanged the clean bowls together in the drying rack. "I don't know what you think is going on," she said. Then she turned around, her face flushed and hot. "Actually, I do know. And you're wrong, anyway, but even if you weren't," she spluttered, looking for the right words. "Even if you weren't—especially if you weren't—I wouldn't come running home to go on a date with Eric or one of Dad's pimply interns, and I find it insulting you would even ask. So you can just—" She felt herself teetering on the edge, hurt and wanting to hurt back.

And then she said it. "You can just go to hell for all I care."

Lane's mom drew back and something shuttered behind her face. "Well," she said. "I think it's time for us to go."

"Yes," said Lane. "I think it is."

Her parents gathered their things and walked out the door. She heard the car start, waited for it to pull away, and then she unlatched the back door and whistled. "Maisie girl," she called, and Maisie yipped in response.

Lane couldn't sleep all night, replaying the fight in her head, worrying about money, worrying about her parents driving home or stopped in a seedy motel on the way. She imagined them kneeling to pray before bed and said her own secret prayer that Hell was a made-up place. She worried, too, that Kit had heard the fight and the accusations, that if she were to find out how Lane felt, something irreparable might be broken between them.

Sitting at the dinner table with her parents, years later, their last words still hung between them. Lane spooned more applesauce on top of her ham. She took big, sloppy bites and licked her spoon clean. She tried to calm herself down. In five years, she thought, she would be so far away. Another country, another planet. She would not even remember how she felt now.

"So, Kit's out of the picture?" Lane's dad asked. He had finished his ham and was dragging his spoon through the leftover applesauce, making patterns on his plate.

"Yes, what happened with all that?" Lane's mom wanted to know.

What had happened? Lane wondered.

Kit had never loved her. There was that. And there had been no check from Lane's parents or commissions in the spring, only an empty bank account, late rent fees. Kit never complained, but came to own Lane's time, her control over their routine growing ever more rigid. Once, when Lane had slept through breakfast, Kit called her a lazy oaf. "You might as well not survive an apocalypse," she said, "with all the use you'd be."

And then one day, Kit had a boyfriend. A guy from the post office. "I didn't know you sent letters," Lane had said, and Kit had just laughed and rolled her eyes. In the spring, Kit and her boyfriend had moved down into the bunker. Kit announced she was getting married. Lane had the house to herself for weeks, and more responsibility than ever with the dogs, but still no money or anything to eat. She lived mostly on peanut butter, eating straight from the jar, sucking on her fingers, no one around to see or hear.

And then the boyfriend was gone, and Kit came back to the house. Started going on runs again and shopping for groceries. Cooking up six eggs every morning. "Power breakfast, Lane, don't forget." Lane smiling, gaining weight again, thinking everything was back to normal.

And then the day, just last week, when Kit went out for a run and came across Bailey, one of the springtime puppies, run over in the road, bleeding out her stomach, covered in blackflies, breath ragged and shallow. "Nothing to do but shoot her," Kit had said. It was the kindest thing, really. They traced back their steps, where they went wrong, and found that Lane had left the gate closed, but unlatched, and only for a minute, while she ran to get a treat for Maisie, and they decided that Bailey must've slipped out then. "Well," Kit had said, like that settled it. Her eyes were pink from holding back tears. She'd handed Lane the gun. "That makes this your job."

Now, at dinner, Lane's parents stared across the table at her. "I don't know," she said, "I guess we just got sick of each other."

"Just like that?" her mom wanted to know. "You were practically in love."

Lane shook her head. "Kit was too much about survival," she said. "There's more to life than that, you know?"

Lane's parents nodded. They looked worried.

"We could still set you up with an intern from my work if you'd like," her dad said. "One of them stands a good chance of getting hired on full-time next year."

"He's cute too," her mom said. "And he plays the piano at church. He's quite good."

"Sure," Lane said, "I guess that'd be alright."

Lane's mom clapped her hands together. "Oh good!"

"So glad you're getting back on track," her dad said. "We'll transfer some money to your account. Maybe you can buy yourself some new clothes."

Lane smiled. "Thank you," she said, and excused herself from the table. She went upstairs into Catherine's room. Her own room had been refurbished into an office space. Her sister's was plastered with photographs. Most of the new ones, right above her bed, were of her and her boyfriend, but tucked between these shots were two from her September visit, so many months ago. The first, a crooked, dim shot of the painting in Lane's old room, soldiers lined up with their gas masks on. And the second, Lane and Maisie, standing in front of the lake, Lane holding a stick high in the air, Maisie jumping up, her paws on Lane's chest.

Lane waited until midnight to get in her car and drive. She parked, three hours later, on the familiar stretch of road that led to the house, that she had run so many times. Her head was thick with sleeplessness. In five years she would remember what all of this felt like. Catherine sipping wine, her parents saying grace, strangers in attack suits and Kit screaming commands, the dogs' leashes rubbing Lane's palms raw. The gun in her hand, its weight, the way it sprang back when she shot. Bailey's puppy feet. The flies feasting on her blood.

Lane entered the yard as silently as she could, but the dogs caught her scent and began to bark, low at first, then louder. By the time she reached the gate, a light had gone on in the house, but it was too late. Lane was calling for Maisie, feeling for her collar. They were running down the road together. Lane's legs were strong, pumping against the pavement. Maisie's tongue was out and Lane's eyes were closed and she knew they would make it, she was sure.

A Temporary Bed

Content Warning: mention of rape

THE NIGHT I MET HIM, he told me I'd be his wife.
"I don't know about that," I said, but he was
persistent.

We were out on the sidewalk.

He was older than me, but he was small enough that I
wasn't scared.

He put his arm around me and we walked into the bar.
"This is the missus," he told the bartender. Some friends
followed me inside. He bought them drinks too. He was
wearing old white pants, stained at the knees, and a satin-
blend sports jacket. "Sit," he said. "Sit, sit." He ushered
us to a table and took the bench seat for the two of us.
The drinks he'd gotten were dark brown and tasted like
birthday cake, sweet and sticky on my teeth.

He said we could call him Neil. "It's not my real name,"
he said, "but it's what people call me." He had run away

from home fourteen years ago. "I'll tell you why another time," he said. "I send money back to my family in the summers."

He walked us most of the way home. The Blue Wave Hostel was at the top of a long hill. He stopped at the bottom and turned to us.

"Goodnight," he said. He hugged me. "Goodnight, honey. Goodnight, my wife." No one had ever spoken to me this way.

"I don't—" I hugged him back and let him walk away.

That was the November I worked the front desk at the Blue Wave and imagined I might never leave. One of the other employees, an older woman named Leslie, had been there eight years already. She wore long, flowing dresses and got all the best shifts, had been an actress in New York, listened to poems on tape and always looked like she had sun on her skin. Her ex-husband, Julian, lived on the island too, in a big house on the mountain with his pregnant girlfriend. Everyone knew Julian. He was always walking through town in a white shirt and prayer beads, little gold hoops in his ears, his girlfriend holding onto his arm with both hands.

Leslie had introduced me from afar. "There's Julian," she'd said. "Pushing seventy and still doing his part to populate the earth."

Julian visited the Blue Wave sometimes. He and Leslie could drink coffee for hours, little bitter cups of it thick with grounds that stuck to the fronts of their teeth. They talked with each other about love, about home, about the daughter they had together who was grown and gone. She told me the men in her life always wanted to talk. "Talk, talk, talk," she said. "Like they're waiting to fall in love with the saddest thing I can tell them."

She called Julian her old friend. "I'm catching up with an old friend," she'd say.

Before he'd moved to the island, Julian had worked in pharmaceuticals, but now, on the island, he was a poet. When he came to visit the Blue Wave, he'd put a Miles Davis CD in, turning it up so that he and Leslie could hear it through the lobby speakers from where they sat in the courtyard. Sometimes he read aloud from poems that he was working on, taking long pauses between stanzas to sip at his coffee, starting up again at the exact moment Leslie had begun to open her mouth, assuming the poem had ended. I eavesdropped on the poems when I could. They were long and full of a horrible kind of intimacy: the way the tendons in his thighs went taut, his older daughter's bellybutton piercing, the sound of his girlfriend peeing after sex with the door wide open for him to hear.

I saw Neil again the day after we first met. "Good morning, my wife," he called out. I looked all around. He was across the street, sitting on the stoop of a dirty white building. He waved me over.

"Hi, Neil," I said. I checked my phone for the time, though I wasn't in much of a rush.

"Come in, come in," he said. He took my hand and pulled me into what turned out to be a shop. "Take anything you want," he said. "Anything for my wife."

I looked around. The shop was dimly lit. There were wire racks of candy and gum by the register. A wooden shelf of sunscreen all the way up to 80 SPF, coconut-scented shampoo, plastic-laminated maps, beach towels patterned in fish, green and pink swim goggles, bracelets strung with plastic beads, big straw hats, and children's swimsuits, red with blue flowers.

I eyed the shampoo.

"You work here?" I asked.

"Almost fourteen years. My boss was my first friend on the island."

"Wow," I said. I looked back at the shampoo.

"Anything you want," Neil reminded me. "Maybe a swimsuit?" He pointed to a child-sized tankini.

I paused. "That's okay." I made a move for the door. "Anyway, I should go."

"Oh no," he said. "If you go I'll be sad." He took my arm in his hand, firmly, so I couldn't pull away. "We'll go for coffee," he said, and led me out of the shop, down the stairs, and into the street.

The bakery was just across from the grocery store. He bought sweet, foamy frappes and set them down on a white plastic table. Just beyond the building I could hear the waves on the rocks. Neil had on the same outfit as the night before, but he seemed more serious now, looking across the table at me, holding his coffee but not drinking.

"Do you like me?" he asked.

I choked a little on my coffee. "Sorry?"

"Do you like me?" he asked again. He tried to lock eyes with me but I glanced down at the table.

"I don't know," I said. I stirred my straw through the brown foam at the bottom of my cup. "Anyway, I should probably go." I stood to leave.

"I can wait," he said. "I can wait for your answer."

On Thursday evening, Leslie and I drove along the coast. Her car was blue, a tin box that only got up to forty miles per hour. The left side of the bumper had been knocked loose and it rattled when the wind came up off the sea.

"It's a wonderful little town," Leslie said. She was wearing a white dress with bell sleeves that draped nearly into her lap, hands clutched at the wheel, silver hair swept beneath a yellow scarf. There was a tremor in her voice that caught at the hard syllables, made them sharper than they already were.

By the time we came into the town, the hills were burning gold. Along the dock the waves splashed high onto our feet. Leslie pointed at a ship with navy paint and polished oak rails. "I was on a ship like that once," she said. Her yellow scarf was coming undone. "The guy I dated after Julian took me on a sailing trip around the world." She smiled up at the boat. "We broke up on that trip, of course."

"You broke up?"

"Oh, sure. I could tell he was getting sick of me, so I asked him, 'Would you rather I wasn't here at all?' and he said, 'Yes, darling, as a matter of fact I would.' He was very British. The trip was a birthday present, though, so I told him we could break up then, but I wanted to complete the route we'd mapped out." She laughed, still looking up at the boat. The sun had begun to go down and the waves were turning black.

"I always know when a man doesn't want me around anymore," she said.

We headed back up the dock to a restaurant with outdoor tables. It was windy, and Leslie offered me her sweater. When I put it on I felt a bit like her, a woman traveling the world on a navy-blue boat. We ordered wine. "Red and white," Leslie said. "We'll have a little of both."

The next morning, Neil was waiting for me outside the hostel. He had hoisted himself up on a low wall, concealed from the entrance behind a lemon tree. "Listen," he said, "it's time for an answer."

"An answer?"

"Do you like me or not?" he asked. "I've waited and now it's time that I know."

I looked down at the ground, then up at the glossy green leaves. I felt very young, scuffing my toes on the dirt path. "Well . . ." I said, looking for the softest way to say it. I hoisted myself up to sit next to him on the wall, feet dangling just above the ground. "I think I'd like to be friends."

"Only friends?"

I hesitated. "Yes," I said, figuring it was true—I could use a friend.

Neil looked away from me, down the street. "Okay." He nodded. "I'll respect that."

"Thanks," I said.

"You know I'm not in love with you or anything," he told me. "I like you, yes, but I'm not in love."

"Okay," I said.

"Good." He had turned back to look at me. "Have you ever been in love?"

"Yes," I lied. "Have you?"

"Oh yes," Neil told me. "The first time I was sixteen. We fell in love and we wanted to get married, but in the end she had to marry someone else. An old man. That was when I left home."

"Because of her?"

"Yes," Neil said. He reached out and took a strand of my hair between his fingers. "And the last time I was in love, I couldn't get out of bed for a whole year. I wanted to die because she'd left me. My boss took care of me, made sure I ate. I couldn't leave the bed. That's why I won't fall in love with you."

I pushed myself off the wall and took a few quick steps backwards. Out from behind the lemon tree, into the open where I could be seen. I'd never heard love talked about like that, like it could ruin somebody's life. "Okay," I said. "We'll be friends."

Leslie and I went dancing that weekend in a big, flat field on top of a mountain. The tree branches moaned in the wind and my hair came loose from its braid, tied itself in knots around my face. Three old men were set up beneath the trees in wooden chairs, two of them plucking at guitars with their eyes closed, a third tuning his violin. There were little cups of whiskey at their feet.

The music started with just the violin, slow and mournful. Leslie and I sat on the ground, facing into the wind, watching the sun go down. Her scarf kept blowing against the tips of my fingers, light and ticklish as bits of meadow grass. She was leaning back, propped up on her elbows, watching the darkest parts of the sky. I kept looking at the side of her face, her high cheekbones lit up with the faintest traces of sweat.

"Leslie?" I asked.

"Hmm?" She didn't look at me.

"Just wondering—" I didn't want to sound naïve. "Just wondering what you think about being in love."

"Oh, I don't know," she said. She was still looking up at the sky. "I've been in love so many times. Or—maybe only a couple of times. Sometimes what feels like love at the time isn't love at all, in the end."

I looked back over my shoulder at the men playing music. The beat was picking up. Someone was going around lighting lanterns. When I turned back, Leslie was sitting up and looking at me.

"You know," she said, "love almost killed me. That's why I came here. This place saved me."

"It did?"

"It brought me back from the brink."

"How?" I asked. I was sitting up all the way now too, hands clasped around my knees.

"After Julian left me, after that British man left me, after so many people had left me—or even after I'd left them—I got to thinking there was no point in any of it. I mean, why bother? I just felt so old." Leslie began tugging at her own fingers, playing with the way her knuckles wrinkled. "I couldn't sleep, but I had a hard time being awake, too. I just got to thinking about the silliest, most horrible things. I would read the news and get fixated on one word, like *nemesis*, and I would spend all day turning it over in my mind. First the sound of it, and then later the meaning. I remember I was lying in bed one night and that word—*nemesis*—it was just pounding out a rhythm in my mind. Like, *nemesis, nemesis, nemesis.*" Leslie patted her thigh, matching the syllables of the words. "I worked in the theater, you know," she said. "And I just felt so washed up. I had—I mean I have—all of this sagging skin, you see, and wrinkles on my neck. And I would touch them and tug on them. And then I got to thinking if I had any nemeses, and god, if they could see me now. I got to thinking that everyone might be my nemesis, whatever that even means." She looked over at me. "It's hard to explain, but I was in a very bad place."

"So you moved here?" I asked.

"Julian bought me the plane ticket, actually," she said. "He was worried about me."

"Julian?"

Leslie nodded. "It's odd, I know. We'd been divorced eleven years at that point. But we've always been close. He knew how bad it was. I think he was one of the only ones who knew." She smiled, shrugging off the strangeness of it all. "By the time I got here, I knew I was never leaving. I sat by the coast every day for a year, as close as I could get without the waves washing over my feet. It didn't matter how cold it got. Sometimes I think that if I ever get sick, I mean really sick, I'll just swim out into the waves and disappear."

"Until you drown?" I asked.

"There's nowhere else I'd rather to die." Leslie wrapped her scarf more tightly around her shoulders. It was night-time now and the sky had deepened. "Let's head back to the music," she said, and got to her feet.

In the center of the field, an old woman and her husband had begun to dance, hands in the air, rotating each other in half circles, little side steps, shoulders dipping low with the movement of their feet. Children ran out and formed a ring around the couple, and then slowly everyone began to join, making wider and wider rings. Leslie and I were way out on the edge, taking little steps side to side with our hands up in the air. I was clumsy, stumbling on pebbles. The circles morphed, faded. I caught glimpses of the old couple, still at the center of the circle. They were holding hands now, spinning, hips swaying. A little boy came up and took my arm, swung me into the rhythm of the dance. His fingers squeezed and loosened, pressing the beat into my arm. He pulled me deeper into the circle until I could just see Leslie through the crowd, the edge of her scarf floating up on the wind, each arm crooked to accommodate a partner.

In exchange for working at the Blue Wave, I had a room all to myself. It was simple, with cold tile floors and white walls, but it had its own bathroom and a hot plate and a plastic filing cabinet that I used as a pantry. There was a TV, too, that had a remote but didn't get any channels, and two twin beds pushed together into one. It was the most space I'd ever had to myself and I did what I could to take care of it, making both beds in the morning, tucking in the sheets at the corners. I found a thin wool blanket in the closet that I spread across both mattresses to create the illusion of a single, large bed. The blanket was gray with a thick blue stripe, the most color in the entire room.

There were windows along one wall that opened with cranks and swung outwards into a patch of pink flowers. Leslie told me, when I moved in, to keep my windows locked at night. She didn't tell me why, just said it like a worried mother and gave me a pat on the shoulder. For all her long dresses, floating scarves, and glasses of wine, she was a nervous person. Though we both lived on the second floor, she kept her windows and doors locked at all times, letting hot air stagnate in her room.

"You have to be careful about your space," she told me. She said she'd learned that in her marriage. "The Blue Wave is the only place in the world where I've had any space of my own," she liked to say, wrapping herself more tightly with her scarf, looking off into the courtyard or beyond the front desk or out across the ocean horizon.

The morning after we went dancing, I was in a daze. I had dried sweat still on my skin. I opened all the windows in my room. I poured thick apricot nectar into a glass and mixed in water, then drank the juice in bed, taking small sips to make it last.

I kept thinking about Leslie on the ferry, looking over the rails to see the water frothing against the boat. Had Julian waited for her at the port? He'd gotten her the plane ticket, after all. Brought her here with no friends, no house, no anything, thinking that he could save her life. I couldn't tell if that was just his arrogance or if that was really love, after all, even if they weren't together. Even if he didn't meet her at the port and she had to walk alone to a hostel on a hill with a white twin bed and a view of the ocean.

A vision of Neil's bed, the one he had laid in for a whole year after his break-up, materialized in my mind. A red blanket, maybe, faded at the hems and tucked under the corners of his mattress. I shivered and pushed the image out of my mind.

It was almost dinnertime and all I'd had was juice. I found some tequila in the cabinet and drank it under the covers, closing my eyes and trying to visualize the mountaintop, the music, that little boy with his hand on my arm. I took big gulps and tried to keep my stomach from clenching too hard around the burn of tequila. Later, I put on fresh underwear, ate a container of strawberry yogurt, got dressed, and went out into the night.

I ran into Jamie, one of the women who worked in the kitchen, and we ended up at a big, empty bar with metal cages set up on the concrete dance floor. A paper sign behind the bar said, "Show your tits for a free shot." Jamie and I were standing up, drinking and moving. I was feeling so warm and light. I kept bumping my hip into hers, just to let her know I was there. Then I was spiraling away out onto the dance floor, trying to move my hips like the old couple on the mountain. Pushing forward just a little, pushing back. The place began to fill up. A woman climbed up into one of the cages and started grinding on the pole in the center. People cheered her on. I cheered her on. A man came up behind me and put his hands on my waist. I could feel his chest on my back and it was warm so I leaned in hard. He spun me around to face him and kissed me, tasting like cigarette smoke. All I could see when I pulled away was his neck.

I thought about this man's bed, what it might look like, and pictured it with the same gray and blue blanket as mine.

What had Leslie said about love again? I spotted Jamie by the bar with her shirt pulled up above her head for the free drink. I laughed and tried to wave.

Cigarette man had me up against a big window now, and he was pressing into me so hard I thought he might bruise my pelvic bones. He took my hand and guided it down his pants. He had loosened his belt. When had he done that? I felt the tip of his hard penis and then I pulled away, ducked beneath his arm, dancing back towards the bar. I sat down on one of the stools. Jamie downed her free shot and passed me her lime to suck on. I tried to picture this place in the morning, with the light streaming in through the big windows, making patterns on the floor.

The cigarette man was back. "Can I buy you a drink?"

I shook my head no, lime wedge still between my teeth.

"Why not?"

I shrugged. He sat down next to me and propped his chin up on his fist, looking at me.

I felt a hand on my arm. The little boy's hand! He was going to show me how to dance!

It was Neil. "C'mon," he said, "we have to go."

I frowned at him. "Why?" I asked, but he just tugged harder on my arm. "Okay, okay," I said, and let him lead me outside. He pulled me down the sidewalk, away from the lights of the bar. He had his face turned away.

"Neil?" I asked.

He didn't say anything.

"Neil, you're scaring me."

No response.

I started to get annoyed. "Can you at least let go of my arm then?"

His fingers dug in harder.

"Let go of my arm!" My voice came out like an indignant child's, high-pitched and pleading. I coughed to cover it up.

"Did you like him? Did you like that man?" Neil asked. I still couldn't see his face.

"No," I said.

"Are you lying to me?"

I could tell that Neil had turned towards me, but it was still too dark to see.

"No," I said again.

"Good." Neil let go of my arm. "He was going to rape you."

"He what?" I said. "How do you know?"

"He was going to lock you in the back of his car and rape you," Neil said. "He saw that you were drunk and he was going to do it."

"He told you that?" My body felt heavy, sinking down into the sidewalk. It was so dark. All I could make out was the shine of his satin jacket, little shapes of light moving in silver flashes.

"He's done it before," Neil said. His voice sounded proud, like he'd backed me into a corner that I couldn't escape. "He has a knife and he would have held it over you while he had sex with you."

I was quiet.

"I could beat him up if you want," Neil offered.

"No," I said. "No, don't do that."

"He told his friends he's seen you around. He told them you'd be easy to get in the car." He put his hands on my arms again, rubbing my shoulders like he was trying to wake me up. "Don't be stupid," he said. "Why are you so stupid?"

"I want to go back now," I said. "I want to go back to the Blue Wave."

Neil kept his hands on my shoulders. "You're so stupid."

"I am not," I said. High, plaintive. I tried to shake myself free but he gripped my shoulders and held me in place.

"It's not your fault," he said. "You're just a child."

"I'm not—"

"You're a child on vacation and I'm an old man."

"You're not that old," I said.

"I'm thirty-nine," he told me. "I bet you didn't know that."

I shook my head.

Neil took his hands off my shoulders. "It's okay," he told me. "I'm not mad at you."

"I think I want to go home now," I said.

"I told that man he was wrong. That you wouldn't be easy like that."

"Okay," I said, "I'm sorry."

When I got back to the hostel, I knocked on Leslie's door. "Leslie?" I said. "Leslie, I need you to tell me again what you said to me on the mountain."

There was no answer, but the next day there was a phone call.

"He's alive," she said. "He's fucking alive."

"Who's alive?" It was afternoon but I was still in my underwear, swallowing back nausea, playing with how my toes looked underneath the sheet.

"Julian," she said.

"What was wrong with him?" I flexed my left foot, then my right.

"No one told you?"

"No."

"He had a heart attack last night," she said. "A bad one." He'd gotten up to get a glass of water in the night and fallen right back over. His girlfriend said he fell back on the bed and then slid down onto the floor like he'd been shot. All three of them had taken the ferry to the mainland, Julian wheeled onboard on a stretcher. "We're at the hospital now," she said. "He's not conscious, but he will be."

"You're on the mainland?" I asked.

"I brought his Miles Davis," Leslie said, "but I forgot to bring anything to play it on." She laughed. "He never would've forgiven me if he'd died without his music."

Leslie stayed on the mainland all week. I didn't see Neil, either. I took on extra shifts, checking people in and out, making restaurant recommendations and tracing paths on an island map with a green pen. I didn't go out much at all. When I did, I took the back roads, cutting away from the coast, away from Neil's shop. Then one night, he was outside the Blue Wave, tucked behind the lemon tree again. Holding a pizza box.

"Would you like to go to the beach?" he asked. He wouldn't look at me.

The moon was bright, not quite full, casting blue shadows on our faces. The sand on the beach was so cold it was almost wet. I tucked my feet beneath me and sat perched, waiting.

"Have some pizza." He still wouldn't look at my face, but he was scrutinizing the rest of me, following the movements of my fingers as I peeled a slice of pizza away from the wax paper at the bottom of the box. The slice was covered in crumbles of blue and white cheese, a sour taste that filled the corners of my mouth with saliva.

He'd brought beer too, and insisted on opening only one can at a time to share. When we had finished the first can he crumpled it in his fist. "Are you mad at me?"

I remembered the way his fingers had felt when he'd called me a child. "No," I said.

"Good. I thought you might be mad." He opened a second can of beer.

"But I didn't like how you talked to me. Before, I mean." My voice came out soft, like I'd asked a question.

"You know I was just trying to protect you," he said, and took a sip. He was smiling now and looking me full in the face. "Let me give you a backrub. I'll make it up to you."

"I'm okay," I said, as though he'd asked me a question.

He shifted in the sand, stretching his legs into an open V. "Come on, I know how to give a Thai massage." He patted the ground between his legs.

"It's really ok," I said. I had no idea what a Thai massage even was.

"First you have to take your hair down," Neil said. He patted the ground again. He was persistent, I had to give him that. I looked around, but there was no one in sight. He scooted behind me, positioning me between his legs. I reached up to unravel my braid. He put his hands on my shoulders and dug his thumbs in hard, moving them in little circles down the length of my back. When he reached the bottom, he moved back up and took my neck in his hands, full circle like he could choke me. Instead, he was gentle. His thumbs traced lines from the top of my spine to the base of my skull, and then his fingers were in my hair, nails scratching my scalp, tugging at my roots harder, then harder still, until my neck bent back to meet his hands.

STREET OF WIDOWS

ELSIE STEPS OUT FROM BENEATH THE AWNING of the Barre Hospital and breathes in the wet, earthy air. She stands a moment, struggling with her umbrella, her curls flattening against her face. Rainwater dampens her gloved fingertips, turning the white cloth grayish and old.

When the umbrella finally springs open she allows herself a moment of relief. Her eyes close and her breathing deepens, damp and raspy. *Henry.* Her eyes open. She begins the long walk home. The rain taps out its rhythm on her umbrella. What will she tell him when he comes home from school? *Tap, tap, tap.* About his father's deep hacking coughs? About the skin that is beginning to tinge blue?

Elsie shakes her head. She won't tell Henry anything just yet. There isn't anything she knows how to say. She passes the bakery, then Aubuchon Hardware. *Robert has always coughed, hasn't he?* She can see him now, stripped down to his undershirt, smoking in the living room. He has always coughed, wiping bits of phlegm from his lips with a handkerchief.

Elsie tilts her umbrella back and looks out at the street. Ahead of her, a dog sits tethered to a signpost, water dripping off the white fur of its beard. It looks up as she approaches, first at her, then at the sky, and begins to whine.

Elsie thinks again of her husband's blue fingertips, splayed out atop his sheets, cold and bloodless. At the hospital, she asked the nurse if it could be frostbite. Silly, she knows now.

Elsie turns and walks back to Aubuchon. There's a line at the counter, but she cuts through and kneels by the chrome gumball machine, slides a penny into the slot, and twists the dial. The gumballs shift and rattle, and one rolls out into the palm of her waiting hand. A white one! A white gumball comes with a prize.

She checks the clock on the wall and sees she's late. Elsie taps the man at the front of the line on the shoulder. "I'm sorry," she says, "but I've won the prize." She holds out the gumball for both the man and the cashier to see. "Do you mind? For my son," she says. She slides the gumball into her pocket and waits while the cashier digs around in a box beneath the counter. He emerges with a red pocket whistle.

Elsie thanks him. The man in line grumbles and shakes his paper bag of nails. "You're welcome," he responds, though she didn't intend her thanks for him.

Back on the street, she walks quickly. The road begins to slope down, away from town. She rounds the corner, comes in sight of the old brick building, and breaks into a run, eyes on the peeling white paint of the front porch. Her umbrella bobs up and down with every step, knocking rainwater onto the skirt of her dress. She reaches the front stoop as the bus pulls to a stop. She can see Henry through the windows, a dark shape moving towards the front of the bus. She takes a moment to catch her breath, to collapse her umbrella, to form a smile.

"Henry!"

He runs to her.

"How was school?"

"How was Dad?"

Elsie pulls the gumball and red whistle from her pocket and gives them to Henry. "Let's go inside," she says, and puts her hand on his back.

He blows once on the whistle, a sharp blast that startles her. He giggles and allows himself to be pushed inside.

Across town, it is Louisa's first night home after three long nights sleeping in a wooden chair, her back rounded and her neck resting on the corner of Luca's bed, huddled there until the nurses sent her out, told her to go home and get some sleep. In bed now, her back aches. The silence of the house feels heavy, like a thing she can touch. When she falls asleep, she dreams of all the noise she is missing. Luca's moaning. Her husband's horrible, racking cough through the years. She wakes up alone, holds her hand up in the darkness and her fingertips are rimmed with blue light. She is careful not to think her husband's name, not to call him back from the dead.

Louisa swings her legs over the edge of the bed and slides into her slippers. She rubs at her knees. They feel swollen, bulbous. Her walk is unsteady.

She has come to understand her husband's death, how he choked on granite dust, just like everybody else. She's lucky she had him for so long, really. None of the men make it much past fifty. It is Luca that she doesn't understand. She kept him out of the quarry, forbade him from stonecutting, found him a job on the farm through a family connection. All the clean air in the world. She was so used to men dying of silicosis, she'd all but forgotten that there were other ways to die.

In the kitchen, she pours a glass of wine and sits at the kitchen table to drink. On the windowsill is a sprouted, molding onion that she has been meaning to throw away. The air is warm and thick with its smell.

Except for raising her glass, Louisa stays as still as possible. Maybe she will be able to fall asleep in her chair, curling her neck to rest at the edge of the table. She thinks of Luca's bed linens and imagines she can hear his breath slowing down, deepening with sleep.

Elsie walks to the hospital the next day, and the day after that. When she thinks of Robert now, she thinks of white beds, of the smell of disinfectant, of nurses in paper hats pressing clean fingernails against his chest. He looks so at home in those beds, knees tenting the crisp linens, face sweating against the thin pillows. Everything at the hospital is new and bright. He likes that, Elsie can tell. It's hard for her to remember him as he was before, coming up the front steps, stomping his boots and clapping the dust from his hands. Laughing. His broad pink fingernails chewed and torn.

Thinking of the dust makes Elsie's throat go dry. She has been a silly and frivolous woman, brushing all that white from his hair, laughing and calling him old man. She thinks of Henry lying on the living room floor, blowing on the prize whistle, his eyes bulged out and watery.

Elsie swings open the hospital door and her heels click against the floorboards. The receptionist waves her on and she goes through another door, into the main chamber, beds lined up against each wall. Everyone is coughing. She stares hard out the window at the back of the room. She wills her mind to go blank, tries not to imagine Robert's lung, pumping like a heart muscle, squeezing out clouds of dust. When she gets to his bed, he's sleeping. Elsie puts her purse on the floor and sits in the wooden bedside chair. She watches the rise and fall of his eyelids, follows their quick rhythm, tapping it out with her fingers against her forearm.

Another woman enters the hall. Elsie watches her pass the line of beds, her eyes fixed on the window ahead of her, the familiar determination not to look at the men dying in their beds. Elsie wonders if she is picturing the lung, the way it contracts. She watches her take a seat next to a boy three beds down. His left leg is missing below the knee. He is sweating. The dressings on the wound look dirty and damp.

The woman bends over him and puts her hands on the wound, moving her fingers across the bandages. Elsie thinks she sees her pressing down with her fingertips, testing the pain. The boy's body goes rigid. When the woman takes a seat by his bedside, Elsie can see that he is short of breath, struggling to talk. The woman gives little smiles that the boy doesn't return. At one point she even laughs. Elsie is startled by the sound it makes in the quiet room. She thinks of Henry's laugh, of Robert holding him ankle deep in the green river.

The woman is wearing a navy dress and matching blazer, buttoned all the way up to the neck. Elsie is sure she's seen the outfit somewhere, *Ladies Home Journal* perhaps, looking very modern on some slim brunette model. On this woman, the dress is unkempt, wrinkled, and it bunches around her round, sloping shoulders. Elsie watches how the fabric moves, how the woman tugs it away from her armpits and readjusts her sleeves.

When the boy begins to nod off, the woman leans in for a last hug, then stands and trails her fingers across the wound, not pressing this time. She seems lost in thought, but after a moment she begins to approach. Elsie looks away, down at the floor, then over her shoulder and back out the window.

The woman doesn't seem to notice her discomfort.

"Silicosis?" she asks, coming to stand beside Robert's bed. She fixates on the blue fingertips and nods, answering her own question. "My husband died of silicosis a few years back. I'm Louisa."

Elsie pauses, then stands up, unsure what to do. "Elsie," she whispers, then clears her throat. "I'm Elsie."

Louisa considers for a moment. "It's a hard way to go, isn't it?" she says. "That's what I remember thinking most—what a hard way to go."

"Yes," Elsie says. "I think that sometimes too."

"But of course, it's the way they all go," Louisa presses on. "Sometimes I think it's worst for those left behind. Do you ever think that? Is that selfish, do you think?"

"No," Elsie says. "No, I'm sure it's not."

"My son's lost a leg. Threshing accident."

"I'm sorry."

Louisa waves the words away. "Do you have a child?"

"A son."

Nodding, she looks down at Elsie's husband, and in the moment of quiet they both listen to the soft rattle of his sleeping breath. Elsie clears her throat to cover the noise. She sees Louisa close her eyes just a beat too long, remembering.

"Listen," Louisa says, "this may be odd, but I'm having a get-together Friday night at my house, if you'd like to come."

"A get-together?" Elsie looks the woman up and down—the rumpled blazer, the dark hair twisted into a knot at the nape of her neck.

"Sure," Louisa says. She fishes in her handbag, extracting a very old and wrinkled calling card. "Here's the address. It's important for us widows to stick together."

Elsie nods and says, "I'll try to make it." It isn't until after Louisa has left, until after Elsie has resumed her bedside post, that she realizes Louisa's mistake.

Friday night, Louisa has pulled the dining table into the kitchen, and in the dining room every chair in the house has been pushed up against the walls. Wooden chairs, plush chairs, even a plank bench from the front porch. On the far wall, a gold-framed portrait of the Madonna. Louisa lines the windowsills with red and white candles, and when she lights them the chairs throw long shadows across the carpet.

The guests arrive after dark. Louisa stands by the door with a jar, collecting seventy-five cents from each woman. Jugs of wine and empty jam jars cover the kitchen table. The regulars pour themselves glasses of deep red wine. They trickle into the dining room and take seats around the edges, sipping in silence and licking their lips.

Elsie is the last, trotting up the front walk, her cheeks flushed. "I didn't figure you lived so far," she pants. She's clutching a tin of almond shortbread beneath her arm like a girl holding her schoolbooks.

Louisa reaches for the cookies. "Thank you," she says, and pulls Elsie inside. Someone has begun to beat out a rhythm on a tambourine. Elsie pokes her head into the dining room. Two women have already begun to dance, elbows linked, stomping out a rhythm around the design at the center of the carpet. A hunched old woman pushes past, carrying a large box. She sets it down on the floor, undoes the clasps, and pulls out a black and gold accordion. "We play music from home," Louisa says. "You'll like it."

At the table, people line up to refill their jam jars. Elsie turns back to Louisa. "I didn't realize that— "

"Welcome to *La strada delle vedove*," Louisa says. "The street of widows is also the street of wine." Someone hands Elsie a glass and Louisa leads her into the dining room. A woman has begun to sing.

"Do you do this every Friday night?" Elsie asks, swaying her hips. Her skirts brush up against Louisa.

Louisa smiles. "Yes, we started before repeal, as a church group, and we'd dissolve those awful fermented wine bricks to use as sacramental wine. Then when I learned how to make the wine myself I suppose we started to drink a bit more and worship a bit less." She laughs. "You'll see. It's a tough break, but you'll be all right." She squeezes Elsie's arm and pushes her farther into the room. They tap their feet in time with the music.

Later in the night, Louisa grips Elsie's arm again. Too tight this time. She stumbles when she does it and uses Elsie's sleeve to pull herself upright. "My son," she says, her eyes wide and watery in their sockets. Her lips dark and stained with wine. "Elsie, what will I do if I lose my son?"

•

To make ends meet, Elsie finds a job at the flower shop downtown, the one in the old white house on the corner. The owner—Betsy—is a spinster who dresses all in brown and smells like watered-down perfume. She knows about Elsie's husband. "There's not much work these days," she warns her when she gives her the job, "but Memorial Day is coming up and Lord knows we've got some graves to cover."

Betsy works in silence. She says she's part of Ikebana, a Japanese tradition, and refers to arranging flowers as "building the bouquet." She's never been to Japan herself, but she's seen pictures in *Travel Agent*. "Imagine pink flowers," she says. "Pink flowers everywhere and little trees that only have leaves at the very top." Betsy even brings in the magazine to show Elsie, the pink flower image spread across two full pages and attributed to a painter from London.

"Before I begin to build," Betsy tells Elsie, "I like to think about the intent behind the bouquet. I try to match it up with a movement I can make with my hand or arm." She closes her eyes, swings her arm out wide, and brings her fingers curling inwards. "Like that," she says. "After I know the movement, I build texture up. It's easy to get distracted by color, but it's the texture that matters."

Elsie tries to understand. She imagines the laundry at home, on the line. Thick carpet, balls of woolen lint on the blankets, strings unraveling from the hems of Henry's pants. She remembers the purple irises she held on her wedding day, petals curling up to touch, like fingers, like bodies. She was so nervous, the flowers wilting in the heat of her hands.

Betsy's favorite flowers are sprigs of tiny white blossoms called baby's breath. She has the seeds imported from Europe. Elsie watches her adding them to her bouquets, humming, explaining, "I'll just round this one out. Lighten it up a bit." She thinks Betsy's bouquets look like soap bubbles, all white and blue and airy, like if she took them out of the vase they might float up into the air and pop.

The first day of April is cold and windy. The clouds hang low. When Louisa opens her door for the newspaper, she finds its pages damp and heavy, though there hasn't been any rain. She brings the paper inside and unrolls it on the kitchen table. "GRANITE WORKERS STRIKE," reads the front page. She looks up, almost calls out for her husband without thinking. Then she catches herself, pulls back. She bows her head and begins reading the article.

Granite workers all across the city are striking. The quarry workers and the granite cutters. The Depression economy, they say, is not an excuse for pay cuts, for layoffs. The leader of the Barre Quarry Workers Union is quoted in the article: "The economy is bad for us too. We will not stand by as owners get rich at our expense, at the expense of our families." He goes on. "The Frenchmen are on our side this time. They have seen the working conditions, and they are on our side."

Louisa reads the article through once, then a second time out loud, just in case her husband has come back to listen. "The Frenchman are on our side," she says. "Would you believe that?" She remembers her husband at the kitchen table, all those years ago, sitting where she sits now, mustache flecked with bits of sauce. "They bring in these damn Frenchmen," he'd said, chewing and talking all at once. "These damn Frenchmen who don't know a thing about working in the quarry, about cutting stone. They think they won't die of the same damn thing as the rest of us? They think they're immune to silicosis?"

Louisa smiled then, and she smiles now, remembering Luca toddling around the kitchen table, arms spread like wings. "Damn," he shrieked. 'The same damn thing!'"

She shakes her head to clear the memory away. She turns back to the article and reads a quote from the mayor. "Can you believe that?" she says. "He thinks this whole thing will blow over if he just gives it enough time."

She imagines her husband's laugh, a dark laugh, as he raises his glass of wine. "To dying in the quarry," he says, and they clink glasses.

She thinks of Elsie, standing in the living room, clutching her jar of wine. Already learning to be a widow. Already learning new ways to live on her own, new ways to fall asleep, new ways to wake in the morning and remember, over and over again. Louisa is more upset about the strike than she thought she would be. It is too late. She pushes the paper aside and shakes her head again.

·

Back at the hospital, Elsie tugs off her gloves and unfurls the paper. "NATIONAL GUARD CALLED IN RESPONSE TO GRANITE WORKERS STRIKE." She glances up at Robert, lying still in his bed, and studies his face. He works his lips as if he might say something, but he is only sucking in air, struggling for breath.

"It's over, isn't it?" she says.

He nods.

"LaPoint says he didn't want the Guard called," she says. "So that's something."

"That's—" Robert pauses for breath. "That's just—" He breaks off into a coughing fit.

"That's what?" Elsie prompts him.

He coughs again, then leans and wipes his mouth on the linens. "That's no better," he says. "That's all." He rolls onto his back and licks at his dry lips.

She blinks at the floor. "But it is a bit better," she says, "that our own mayor isn't against us."

He opens his eyes and looks at her, starts to speak, then closes his mouth. "How is Henry?" He pauses and ducks his head, catching his breath. "I haven't seen him since—" More coughing.

Elsie's cheeks flush. "I just—" she says, then pauses to wait for the coughing fit to pass. She leans away from the back of the wooden chair and readjusts her skirts. Her husband finishes coughing, then looks back at her. "I just," she starts again. "I just wasn't sure if he would be ready to see you," she says. "I think some things might come as a shock." Robert is breathing hard. She looks, rather pointedly, at the horrible deep blue of his fingertips.

"You coddle him," Robert says. "He's got to find out somehow."

"I just thought—"

"I'm not getting better. He's got to find out somehow." He lies back, breathing hard, and closes his eyes again.

Elsie nods. "I know, I'm sorry."

She smiles at him, does not read him the last paragraph of the article, the part about cutbacks, about management rolling back free medical care.

The next time Louisa visits, she finds that a nurse has pushed Luca's bed into the far corner of the room to clean and drain his wound. She is sweating into her paper hat, and a paper mask is pulled tight across her nose and mouth. Her hair is white around the edges and is coming undone in curls around her face. As Louisa gets closer, the smell hits her. The nurse pulls the bandages away from the boy's leg, revealing ground-up, rotting flesh. She can still see a bit of white hipbone glinting through the mess. She can hardly imagine that this is her son, sweating and green with infection. She remembers him coming home from the farm, big black eyebrows drawn together as he squinted into the sun. His cheeks had flushed such a deep shade of red—almost purple. Now there is blood on the bandages and its smell, like old metal, bites the back of her throat. She swallows hard and covers her mouth with a handkerchief as the nurse dabs at the wound with a hot compress. Pale yellow pus oozes out.

"Luca," Louisa says. She is touching his arm but he doesn't wake up.

"We've given him something for the pain," the nurse explains. She begins to rewrap the wound, refusing to look at Louisa even when she speaks. It's a bad sign. Nurses stopped making eye contact in the weeks before her husband died, too, when his hands were blue and they had to pump the breath from his chest.

As Memorial Day draws closer, Betsy and Elsie are kept busy in the shop. A shipment of roses must be transplanted into painted clay pots. There are trays of lily bulbs with their pointed green leaves spearing up through the earth, gladiola stems to clip, iris buds to water, and tiny potted violets to arrange in the windows. There are plants that Elsie has never seen before: spiky little shrubs, thick-leaved succulents, orchids that arrive looking like old twigs, which need to be fed with bits of ice, which Betsy promises will blossom into creamy purple and white flowers.

When Memorial Day arrives, all of La strada delle vedove turns up at the flower shop. A parade of women dressed in black, and by now Elsie knows them all. Louisa arrives at noon, wearing a hat with a black veil pinned to the brim. She picks a pot of dark red roses for her husband's grave and, when Elsie shows her the succulents, she buys a small one for the windowsill by Luca's bed.

At the end of the day, Betsy lets Elsie take home an orchid, a dead-looking stick, wired upright in a pot of mulch. "It really will bloom," she insists. "Let me know when it does."

At home, Elsie puts the orchid in Henry's room. "It really will bloom," she tells him and kisses him on the forehead. When he falls asleep, she knocks on the neighbor's door to let them know she's going out, then heads north up the street towards Louisa's house.

She can see the red and white candles burning in the windows as she approaches, but hears none of the usual noise. Inside, Louisa is still wearing the hat with the veil. Elsie has to squint to make out her eyes. Louisa waves Elsie away towards the wine table. "No fee tonight." It is crowded, and the women are drinking heavily. Someone pours a glass for Elsie. In the dim lighting, the wine looks black in her cup.

Later in the night, Louisa leads the women through her dining room and into the parlor, a small space with dark wooden cabinets, a gold rug, and a grand piano. Elsie stays by the doorway, eyelids drooping, slipping into a haze. A woman sits at the piano and begins to play, then sing. Her mouth is stained dark with wine. Louisa joins in next, her voice low and raspy. *Io vó narrar con grato cuor.* Elsie knows the song but not the words. *Amazing Grace, how sweet the sound.* More women join in. Their voices rise to meet one another.

Elsie turns, goes into the next room for more wine.

The voices grow distant. It is a funeral song, she knows, and in her mind she can see her husband's body doubled up, wheezing.

By October, after Elsie has missed her rent payment three times, she comes home to a yellow note tacked to her door. She has a week to get out. Her landlord won't look at her when they pass in the hallway. He fixes his gaze on his wirehair fox terrier, who is nosing at Elsie's skirts, and mumbles, "Times are hard," as though she might not have known.

At night, Elsie dreams about the yellow paper. She is in a dark room, watching the paper drift across her line of sight. It goes back and forth, lit up with a faint glow. Little folds at the corners open and close like winking eyes. She tries to wink back but can no longer close her eyes. She can't open them either. They recede backwards into her skull until she can no longer see the paper, until she can no longer see anything at all.

She wakes to music and lets her eyes adjust, lets them take in the gray of the nightstand, the black shadows around the edges of her pillows. The music outside is high and thin. She imagines it whistles from the long tendrils of the weeping willow across the street.

She gets up and goes to the window. A quiet night, no wind. Henry is splayed on his back in the front yard. His arms are raised to his face, hands cupped, as though he is calling out into the night. The notes of his song dip low, then swing back up. She isn't sure if he's crying or not. After a moment she calls to him to come inside, go back to sleep.

In the morning, Elsie folds up the yellow paper as small as she can and slips it inside of her glove. All the way to work, it scratches against the underside of her wrist, and all day long it rests against the finger holes, tucked into the sleeve of her sweater, hanging at the back of the shop.

She spends the morning transplanting begonias. Their roots look like pink and white worms. She swirls her finger twice in each pot, then presses the tuber in and packs it with dirt. When she's done, she sprinkles each one with water and lines them up in the window-sill. Betsy says they look like children headed off to school and Elsie has a sudden, quick vision of Henry lying in the dark grass, singing.

Betsy has brought a cheese and lettuce sandwich for lunch, and she gives half to Elsie. They sit outside on the porch to eat, knees tucked up on the front steps. It's a clear day, and they both look out at the sky. Betsy starts to speak, then smiles, then starts again. "Do you ever think the sky looks like the lens over an eye?" she asks. "That layer you can see from the side, if you look carefully in the right light?" She's staring at Elsie now, but Elsie keeps looking out at the sky.

"We're being evicted. We have a week to find some-where new to live."

Betsy looks away.

"I'm not asking for help." Elsie wishes she hadn't said anything at all. "I just wanted to tell someone, that's all."

"You haven't told anybody else?" Betsy glances over, then away again.

Elsie shakes her head. "I don't think I'll tell Robert. I don't want that on his mind when he dies."

They don't talk much for the rest of the afternoon. Betsy stands at the counter and makes her soap bubble bouquets, her nervous fingers plucking at the baby's breath, fluffing up the petals like she would a pillow. At the end of the day, she helps Elsie carry home some of the wooden crates from the storeroom to use for packing. They are rough and full of splinters, damp in the bottom and stuck all over with leaves. They line them up in Elsie's front yard to dry.

Louisa's hands are purple and red when she answers the door. "Elsie," she says and wipes her hands dry on her apron, leaving behind streaks of color and bits of pulp. "What are you doing here?"

It's midday. The sun is bright behind Elsie's back. She shifts from one foot to the other. "We've been evicted," she says. "Or we're going to be."

Louisa opens the door farther and stands aside to let Elsie in. "How long do you have?" She closes the door. The light dims.

"Three days. Friday's our last day."

Louisa nods. She goes back into the kitchen and Elsie follows. On the counter is a giant glass bowl full of mashed grapes. "Would you like to help?" Louisa asks. She gets Elsie an apron and shows her how to squeeze the juice from the skins without making a mess. They stand over the bowl, side by side, squeezing the grapes.

"I never knew this was how you made the wine," Elsie says.

"How did you think I did it?" Louisa laughs.

Their hands and wrists are red. Their fingertips absorb most of the color and become a deep purple.

"I have room here if you'd like," Louisa says, and Elsie, without thinking, reaches to hug her, dripping grape juice down the back of her dress.

Henry moves into Luca's room, sleeping in the lower level of a trundle bed. The upper level is laid out with trinkets and toys, gifts and prayers for Luca. Elsie sets up Henry's crate on its side, like a wardrobe, and puts the orchid on top. She feeds it ice chips regularly, though it still looks very much dead. Even Henry has taken to watering the twig, filling tin cups and bringing them into his bedroom, using his fingers to sprinkle water down near the roots.

Luca's bedroom is nicer than anything Henry has ever known. He spends long hours sitting on the soft carpet or wrapped up in Luca's down comforter, tuning the radio to different stations. His favorite show is *Believe it or Not!* He loves to listen to Ripley stuttering out odd facts. "Lindbergh wasn't the first man to cross the Atlantic," Henry reports over dinner. "Sixty-six people went before him. Did you know?" And another night, "Ripley told me about a railroad man who survived an accident in Cavendish where a metal rod went all the way through his head." He pokes his knife into his chin, aimed straight up through his jaw, to illustrate. Then, "I heard about a father and son who each lost a leg. Do you know what they did then?" Elsie and Louisa didn't know. "They shared shoes," Henry said. "*Believe it or not!*"

On several occasions, Elsie catches Louisa at night, looking in at Henry asleep in the trundle bed. She figures she's imagining him as Luca, and she doesn't bring it up.

On a Saturday, Elsie goes into Henry's room herself. "I'm going to the hospital if you'd like to come."

He grins. "Can we bring him a sandwich? Can we bring him a glass of wine?"

"He doesn't eat much," Elsie tells him. "He's got a stomachache."

"All the time? He's got a stomachache all the time?"

She nods. She doesn't know how to say the rest, but she figures that he'll see for himself. Skinny, blue fingers, wheezing gasps. The whole way to the hospital she indulges herself in a fantasy that when they walk through the doors, Robert will look young again, and healthy, Henry saved from a final image of his father as a twisted gray ghost. He'll have nightmares, she knows, for weeks.

Luca dies on a Sunday. Louisa is not there when it happens, but Elsie and Henry are. She sees the nurses gather around the bed, check his pulse, mark something down on a clipboard.

"What's happening?" Henry asks. "What's happening to Luca?"

Elsie shushes him. "Louisa wouldn't want you using his name."

In the flower shop, Elsie clips the ends off of red, pink, and yellow gladiolas. She sticks her nose into the center of a blossom and breathes in deep. The smell of mud in the store has become unbearable. The back of her throat is swollen and raw.

When she finishes pruning the gladiolas, she begins trimming pieces of greenery, draping them over the sides of the counter like hanging vines. She plucks out bits of fern and grass that have gone brown and brushes them off onto her skirt. Then she adds lavender larkspur, just a few pieces at either end of the bouquet.

Louisa hasn't slept in the two days since her son's death. Elsie saw her in the morning, hunched over the kitchen table, gripping a full cup of water between her two hands. She hadn't moved all night—except perhaps to refill the cup—staring up at the beams in the ceiling, blinking and blinking, following the cobwebs from one side of the house to the other.

The purple against the green is calm, like late spring, like nice soap, like a bruise that has begun to heal. Elsie adds yellow and pink lilies. Their mouths hang forward, open wide. She will bring the bouquet for the top of Luca's casket.

She sticks pink roses in, then long strands of bells of Ireland, adds baby's breath and tiny blue forget-me-nots, more ferns, a stalk of yellow gladiolas. The bouquet builds out in front of her, heaped on the counter. She adds more roses—darker and purple. They remind her of Louisa's eyes, deep and hollow, rolling slowly upwards. She will bring the flowers to the funeral. It is the best she can do.

At Night

H<small>ER</small> <small>EYES</small> <small>OPENED</small> <small>SLOW</small> <small>AND</small> <small>BLURRY</small> into the afternoon sun. Her pillow was warm, and she moved closer to it, wrapping it in her arms. Her skin felt soft and old. The fruit of her might slide right out. *Today. Today is the day.* She was almost sure of it. "Today's the day," she said out loud. Someone came to her bedside and patted the top of her hand. "Today," she insisted. "The fruit of me is coming out." More patting. It was too great an effort. She moved back into the pillow, closed her eyes against the light.

She was in her old bed in the old room. She twisted her fingers into the hem of the blanket. There were pale brown bloodstains somewhere, somewhere. She was too warm. She was sweating. *I am going to die, I am going to die.* "I'm too warm," she said, struggling against the weight of the blanket. Someone pulled it from her. The sun was low and orange on her lap. Her skin wet like a new flower. She pressed her toes back into the warmth of the blanket and turned to look for the shape next to her, for breathing, for the lump of his back turned away. It was a mistake. He had gone. She cried out. Figured why not scream, why not speak in wild verse. It didn't matter, did it? She had had her life, her job, her kids, her husband's head going bald in the palm of her hands.

She had dreamt about her grandfather dying on a cot in the living room. She was seventeen. She was inside his body when he died, and she felt him go cold. He had wanted to die, had called her on the phone and said, "It's time." She was seventeen and it was a hard dream to wake up from. She rolled over and held her boyfriend's hand. He made a noise in his sleep that sounded like "Okay."

It was nighttime now, but someone was still there. It was Ben, asleep in the chair by her bed. He had left the lamp on. She tried to call out to him, but he didn't open his eyes. She felt like she needed to tell him something. About the blood that had come before him, all the blood that had come out of her. She had sat on the toilet and let the blood run and she had heard her husband open the door in the hall, home now, and still she had not been able to raise her voice to tell him what had happened.

"You came next," she said to Ben and didn't care that he couldn't hear. She wanted to tell him how nice it was that he had been there, that he had lived, that he was sitting there now, skin golden from the lamplight. It was too hard. Her words stuck and her breath caught. *This is it. This is it.*

She waited for it to come, imagined she could feel her feet cooling down, all of her skin cooling down. She thought it might be like fainting, like black and gray edges that closed down around her vision. It was coming now, she knew, and she saw the lamplight flicker and expand, out and out, until all she could see was yellow.

She tried to reach for Ben's hand, but it was too far. She wanted to die with all her good thoughts, all the people she loved. She tried hard to think. Her husband's hands pressed deep in the sand, looking for shells with his eyes closed into the wind. Ben's voice reading aloud his school papers from the chair in the kitchen. The yellow walls and the cracks in the ceiling. Her first home. Red tiles. She had gotten so many bloody noses as a child. The doctor had wanted to cauterize a gland in her nose. Cauterize it! She could not hold everything in her heart at once. Her mother had clipped her fingernails until she was seven years old. *Thank you.* She tried to die with those words in her mind. *Thank you thank you thank you.*

It was too hard. The lamplight subsided. She remembered the red walls of a friend's house, or maybe an aunt's. Where had she been? She thought of plums. God, how she would love a plum. There was something cold deep in her throat. Maybe she should have prayed while she had the chance. She reached out one more time, to Ben, to the lamplight. It was time. Why had it not happened yet? Her vision was brown around the edges, brown like the stains on the blanket. She hoped it wasn't silly, dying like this at night. She wanted to tell Ben what was happening, but it was too difficult, and anyway, it was too late. There was a tugging sensation, like a long, coiled rope pulled from her insides, slowly up and out of her throat. She coughed once, and kept her mouth open to let it pass.

DINNER PARTY

CLAIRE HAD GOTTEN IN LATE THAT EVENING, her mom already asleep upstairs, her dad shuffling through the house in his flannel robe, unlocking the door for her. Now, lying in her childhood bed, she thought of her parents across the hall. Every time she saw them they were older than she expected, new shadows and new wrinkles. She wondered what her mother would look like now. The lights in Claire's bedroom were out, but she had kept the door open just a crack and her dad had left the hall light on. She lay awake for a long while, looking at the yellow stripe the light made against the edge of the doorframe.

When Claire went downstairs in the morning, she found her dad on the screened porch. He was eating a banana with a paring knife, peeling back the skin bit by bit, slicing off pieces of the fruit and bringing them up to his mouth still balanced on the blade. Pushed into the corner of his plate were a handful of pills in different shapes and sizes, and she watched from the doorway as he swallowed them in between bites, washing them down with a single sip of apple juice. *Banana, pill, apple juice,* went the rhythm. *Banana, pill, apple juice.*

"Good morning," Claire said, stepping out onto the porch. Her dad gave a little start and swallowed his bite of banana too fast.

"Oh," he said. "I didn't hear you come downstairs." He pulled the peel back up around the banana and set it on his plate. "Let's see what we've got for breakfast." He made his way into the kitchen.

She followed. "Don't worry about me. I'm not even hungry."

Her dad ignored her and opened the fridge. "Well, we don't have much." He pulled out the apple juice and a half gallon of milk. In the pantry he found some digestive crackers and a half-eaten box of Cheerios from her last visit, six months earlier. "And you're welcome to the bananas too," he said, laying everything out on the counter in front of her. "I'm sorry it's not much to choose from."

"It's plenty," Claire said. She fixed a plate of sliced banana and digestive crackers and poured herself a glass of milk.

Her dad stayed in the kitchen and watched. "Take as many crackers as you want," he told her. "We've got another pack in the pantry."

She kept her back turned for a moment after she poured the milk. "Is Mom still sleeping?"

She heard her dad's quick breath, his pause, and then he came up behind her and took the milk. "Yes," he said. He put it back in the fridge. "She hasn't been feeling herself lately."

After breakfast, Claire's dad went upstairs to answer some e-mails. She stood in the kitchen and listened to the slow creak of his steps, the sound of the office chair rolling across the confines of its hard plastic mat, the bright ascending note of the computer starting up.

She went into the living room and put both hands and her head on the bookshelf. She had that dizzy feeling, her body beginning to reel backwards in time.

She hadn't seen her cousin Robbie yet—even her parents hadn't heard from him all week. Claire knew this would be the hardest thing. They never saw each other anymore. He'd gotten tall and strange, his mouth turned down at the corners, bottom lip bitten in, tugged under and hidden.

Once, when she was seven or eight, she'd been in the front yard catching fireflies with Robbie. It was dark and the grass was cool beneath her feet. He had tried to snatch them in the air, clapping his hands after their quick, blinking lights. Claire had knelt down low and trapped them where they landed, slow and dark, just beetles on the ground. She'd held out her cupped-together hands, opening them just enough for Robbie to press his eye between her thumbs and see the bug flashing against her skin. She imagined it blinking in panic and opened her hands, releasing the firefly into his face. He screamed and ran. The porch light flicked on.

Claire tried to remember who had come to the top step of the porch, Aunt Reese or her own mom, maybe both the sisters at once. Just a voice calling out, "Play nice."

She'd hardly thought of him since her college graduation, four or five years now, but his face came pressing at the backs of her eyelids. He'd been small for his age, with pale, thin skin like wet paper pressed up against his bones, but his features had been full and pretty. Long lashes, dark eyes, lips dry and bloodied red from chewing. Claire had envied his mouth when they got older, the way he could tug and pinch his bottom lip into a pout.

One time, Claire had helped Robbie pick all the tomatoes out of his mom's garden and throw them—*splat*—against the overturned wheelbarrow. "My mom's a slut," he'd told her. She hadn't known what that meant. "It means she invited my gym teacher over for dinner and let him spend the night," he said.

"Spend the night?" She considered the gym teacher's green mesh shorts, the way they rode up the insides of his pale, hairy thighs.

"In her *bed*," Robbie said.

Claire thought she understood, and threw more tomatoes against the hull of the wheelbarrow. Her favorite were the yellow ones, big and gushy, with seeds that slid down into the grass and a thick, mealy flesh.

Aunt Reese had cried when she'd seen her crushed tomatoes. Claire's mom had been furious. "Don't you know how hard it is to grow a tomato?" she'd scolded, right in front of Robbie and Aunt Reese. Claire's cheeks had flushed. She hadn't known. "Don't you know how long it takes?" her mom had yelled. "How much care you've got to give them if you want them to survive?"

For lunch, Claire's dad made up plates of ham and cheese roll-ups and a few slices of lettuce. "No bread," he apologized. He brought a plate upstairs to the bedroom and, hiding in the stairwell, she heard him murmuring, "Honey, just one roll-up. That's all I'm asking." There was a pause. Claire could only just make out the faint impression of her mom's voice. "Yes, she's right downstairs," she heard her dad say. Another pause, her mom's faint whispering. Then, "Of course she asked about you."

After lunch, Claire drove to the store. She needed to get out of the house. Her head was starting to feel heavy, her legs weak. Her dad had taken more pills with lunch: *ham, pill, water, ham, pill, water.* A deep sigh stuck and rattled in his lungs. *Ham, pill, water.*

"That one's a nice color," Claire said, pointing to a particularly large, burgundy pill.

"I suppose it is," he'd said, and made sure to swallow it next.

While she was out, Claire bought a black dress for the funeral. The one she picked was long and linen with three big wooden buttons sewn onto the breast. It was from a store that was probably too old for her, and the dress was so shapeless it hardly touched her body at all, but she had been feeling that kind of old lately, that kind of shapelessness inside her own skin. The dress felt right. It felt like how she imagined her mom, lying upstairs in bed, taking bites of deli ham and resting her puffy face against the corner of her pillow. Like the hard lump you might get in your throat from swallowing food lying down. Thin skin on veins. The round bones of knuckles.

Aunt Reese had always had pretty hands. Her fingers were long and slender, her skin smooth. She'd worked as a hand model for a nail polish company for fifteen years. There was a picture of her hands on a plastic advertisement at the drugstore, one hand poised in mid-stroke above a glossy orange fingernail.

She always wore gloves when she gardened.

Claire could remember going with her mom to visit Aunt Reese the first time the gym teacher left her, bringing over groceries and a few bag lunches for Robbie. He had answered the door without a word, looking straight past Claire and her mom out into the front yard. Then he'd gone and sat at the kitchen table, rubbing the scabs on his knees, not responding when Claire asked him if he wanted to go play. It was afternoon, but Aunt Reese was still in bed. She'd rubbed her blue eye shadow almost to the tips of her ears, streaked and faded like a bruise. Her eyes were red. Black lines of mascara had built up along the sides of her cheeks where she had been wiping her tears with the backs of her wrists.

Claire's mom had cried too. She'd gone over and gotten into bed with Aunt Reese, holding her head and stroking her hair. "It's okay," she said, over and over. "It's okay. It's okay." Claire had stood in the doorway and looked at Aunt Reese's hands, lying on top of her blanket with the fingers splayed out. They were clean and fresh looking. Her fingernails were shining like little pink shells. Claire wondered if the gym teacher would miss Aunt Reese's pretty hands. Aunt Reese had stopped crying. She was taking deep breaths and looking up at the ceiling. Claire wanted to say something then, but she kept quiet, thinking of the tomatoes, remembering how little she knew about taking care of someone else.

The gym teacher had come back, the first time with an apology, the next time a red rose, and the time after that he'd brought a whole bouquet of roses, red and white with all the thorns pulled off. Aunt Reese had tied the roses together with twine and hung them upside down in the kitchen window. "So they can last forever," she'd explained. She'd let Claire feel how the roses held their brittle paper shapes.

Claire's mom hadn't been impressed by the roses. Claire had heard her telling Aunt Reese, "Well, if it's roses you want, I'll buy you some damn roses." But Claire could see how beautiful they were, even brown and fragile, even flaking away in her palm.

The fluorescent lights in the grocery store made Claire's eyeballs ache. She had to stop in the cereal aisle, and then again near the salad dressings, to cup her hands over each closed eye and take in the darkness. She tried to remember Robbie's favorite food. In the end, she bought ingredients for lasagna and a salad, a box of granola, more milk, eggs, some canned soup, a loaf of oat nut bread.

In the parking lot, she closed her eyes again and tried to track her breathing. The bags of groceries were in the backseat, belted in like they might get hurt. Claire pulled her phone out of her pocket. She was so tired of waiting. She reclined the car seat, unlocked her phone, and called Robbie. She couldn't remember the last time she'd talked to him over the phone—maybe never.

"Who's this?" he asked when he picked up.

"It's me, Claire." She held the phone away to clear her throat. "Just wanted to let you know that my parents and I are having lasagna tonight around 6:30 and you're welcome to come over. I mean, if you want to. If you like lasagna."

Robbie hesitated. "Ok," he said. "Ok, I'll try to make it."

Claire held the phone away again and took a deep breath. "Well, good," she said. "It'll be nice to see you again."

"Ok," Robbie said. It sounded like he was holding the phone away from his mouth too, his voice fading away when he spoke.

"How have you been?" She chewed her tongue between her teeth. What a ridiculous question.

Robbie didn't say anything.

What a terrible, obvious question.

"I'm sorry," Claire said. She wondered if he had set the phone down entirely. "I mean—that was the wrong question. I can't imagine what you're going through. I just wanted to make sure you're okay." The words came out in a rush. She could feel her ears turning hot.

"I'm fine," Robbie said.

Claire was startled by his voice. "Oh," she said. "Okay, well, I'll see you tonight." She hung up the phone and leaned her head against the window, pressing her burning ear against the cool of the glass. She never knew if she'd done the right thing.

When Robbie got his license, he'd bought an old blue Subaru with a big dent in the passenger-side door. Claire could remember the day because he'd shown up outside her house, honking the horn until the whole family came outside. It was the first night of the county field days, and he had driven her in his new car, parking a half mile away from the entrance to avoid the muddy parking lot. Robbie had spent all his money on the car, so Claire had paid to get them onto the swings. They'd started slow and then picked up speed, twirling in a wide circle, lifting high above the crowds. "Spread your arms out," Claire had shouted into the wind, and he'd done it, the two of them with their arms out like wings, lifting whole inches out of their seats. He had screamed and then laughed, a harsh yelp that came clawing its way out of his throat.

One week later, Robbie had driven the Subaru straight into the gym teacher's mailbox. The gym teacher wasn't home when it happened. He was standing in Aunt Reese's kitchen, leaving her for the last time. The hood of the car had crumpled, the front headlight cracked down the middle, and the mailbox came up out of the ground, the buried block of cement exposed in the road and crawling with worms.

"Kid sure knows how to express himself," Claire's dad had said, and she had felt a sudden, overwhelming gratitude for him. He had hitched Robbie's car to the back of his truck and towed the wreck home. The car had sat in the driveway, dented and rusting, long after the gym teacher was gone.

When Claire got home with the groceries, her dad was asleep in the living room. His eyelids were wrinkled up, squinting even in his sleep. Her chest felt tender and sore. She laid a blue fleece blanket over her dad's lap, holding her breath to keep from waking him. Then she turned and left the room, past the bookshelf with its gold-embossed photo albums, labels handwritten on white stickers. "Myrtle Beach," "The Old Cabin," "Claire Age 6-10."

Claire took the stairs up to the landing, paused, went

all the way to the top. She could hear her mom snoring behind the door. She went in.

The headboard was pushed up against the left wall, the bed protruding into the center of the room. Claire could just see her mom's hair above the top of the blanket, white spider silk across her blue pillowcase. A pair of khakis had been left on the floor, belt still hooked through the loops. She bent to pick them up, hang the belt in the closet, fold the pants on top of the dresser.

The far wall was covered in photographs that leaned forward in their frames. Claire moved closer. She recognized her dad, young, laughing. Another of her parents kissing. She checked behind her to make sure her mom was still sleeping, as if she could be caught with all these memories. In another picture, a large one with a thin black frame, a young Claire was holding onto Aunt Reese's hand. Robbie was on his mother's other side, clutching his whole body up against her leg. Both Claire and Robbie had turned their heads away from the camera—a secret look hidden by Aunt Reese's blue jeans.

Claire turned back into the bedroom. "Mom?" she said. "Mom?"

Claire's mom woke with a gasp and sat straight up in bed. "I'm here," she said, breathless. "I'm here. I'm awake."

Claire sat on the edge of the bed.

"Oh, Claire, it's you," her mom said. "I'm sorry I haven't seen you yet, I've just been . . ." She gestured at the blankets on the bed.

Claire said it was okay. Her mom's face looked wrinkled, ancient. Claire tried not to stare. "Are you coming to Aunt Reese's funeral?" she asked, voice lowered to a near whisper.

Her mom's face drooped a little more. "Of course," she said, but she lay back down when she said it, like even the thought was too much for her.

Claire nodded. She smiled. She reached halfway to take her mom's hand, then let her arm fall heavy onto the bed between them.

"You'll be okay," said Claire. "We'll all be there." On the bedside table there was another photograph, an old Polaroid of her mom and Aunt Reese as little girls, curled up like cats beneath the Christmas tree.

Claire took a deep breath. "Mom," she said, "I'm making lasagna for dinner, and I've invited Robbie to come."

Her mom nodded. "I'll do my best," she said, and folded the blankets down to her waist, hands flat and palms down against the small rises of her thighs.

Claire had wrapped the lasagna in tinfoil and was keeping it warm in the toaster oven by the time Robbie showed up. He was skinny and so pale that his pinched-together lips were barely tinged with pink. He had a boy with him, who he said liked to be called M. "My girlfriend's kid," he said. "I'm babysitting." M looked at Claire and bared his teeth like a dog.

Claire hugged Robbie. "I'm so glad you're here."

Robbie didn't say anything, but he did return the hug. Claire took this as a good sign. "I think it's important to be with family during times like this," she said. M snickered. Claire shot him a look, her face still pressed sideways against Robbie's chest.

Claire led them into the dining room. She set a fifth place, poured a glass of milk for M and a glass of wine for Robbie. Her dad was already in his seat, fussing with his pills. He looked up when Robbie entered and called out his name like a sports announcer. "Robbie!" he said. "It's been a while."

"Sorry about that," he mumbled, looking down at the floor. He sucked in his bottom lip and reached for M's shoulder, guiding him into his seat.

In the kitchen, Claire waited near the stairs and listened. Nothing. In the next room, M was asking what the pills were for.

Claire took the tinfoil off the lasagna and carried it out with hot pads. She brought out the salad, plates, bowls. Still no sound from upstairs. She filled a glass with water anyway and set it in the corner of her mom's placemat. "Help yourselves," she said. She could feel herself smiling a big, horrible smile. "Robbie?" she said, pushing the salad bowl his way.

He filled his plate. M slouched in his chair and gnawed at the edge of the table. "If my mom died of cancer, I wouldn't be eating lettuce," he said. He clasped his hands and put them on top of the table. Robbie ignored him.

He pushed the salad in M's direction, then poured ranch dressing into his bowl and mixed it around with his fork.

There was a sound on the stairs. Claire's mom came into the room, smiling, one hand on the wall. Claire's dad shifted in his seat like he wanted to get up, to help her to her chair. Instead he stayed put. "You're up," he said. The skin around her eyes was blue, purple, green. Little veins that pulsed. She sat down in her chair and bowed her head.

"Who are you?" M asked.

Claire's mom squinted into her lap like the question was a bright light.

Robbie told M to shut up and eat his lasagna. He poured a second glass of wine. His jaw was twitching.

Claire put food on her own plate, took a breath, a bite, a sip of wine. There was a light sweat building along her hairline. She tried to focus. *Breath, bite, sip of wine. Breath, bite, sip of wine.* Building little rhythms in the long stretches of silence. Grinning. Thinking of the tomatoes in the garden, of the release when their insides burst open on the lawn.

FOR AVA

FIRST, I'LL TELL YOU ABOUT THE HOUSE I grew up in, big and painted a dirty shade of red. The lawn scrubby, full of sticks, more moss than grass. My mother worked for Avon, a multi-level marketing company. She bought makeup in bulk from the company, went door to door trying to sell it to the neighbors. She was always getting new shipments in—boxes and boxes of waterproof eyeliner, liquid foundation, lip gloss, mascara, cuticle cream, nail polish, brushes, face wipes, anti-aging cream, and, my favorite, bronzing pearls, which looked like rabbit poop but broke apart when I touched them into a fine gold dust. My mother bought more makeup than she could sell, lining the walls of whole rooms with boxes, sometimes two deep, sometimes blotting out light bulbs or covering entire windows so that inside, our big house felt very small and dark.

The trouble with my mother was, she wasn't the kind of woman people wanted to buy makeup from. She wore too much on some parts of her face and not enough on other parts. She wore stretched-out turtlenecks and always the same pair of green sweatpants, kept her hair dyed a bizarre shade of burgundy, double-knotted her sneakers. She used unscented shower products, never smelled like flowers or vanilla. She slept in a different bedroom than my father. In fact, they slept in entirely different halves of the big red house. She kept the thermostat on her half at fifty-five. He couldn't stand the clutter of the Avon boxes. They said they loved each other better that way, with some space between them.

I was the middle child of three sisters, or so I thought until, parked outside the bowling alley on a playdate with two of my closest friends, my mother revealed that because she had frozen her eggs, I was actually, technically speaking, the oldest. My egg had been frozen the longest.

At that point in my life, my mother had already taught me about sperm and eggs, the basics of baby making, but one of my friends, May Ellen, asked, "What do you mean Lucy came from an egg?" to which my mother responded with an answer so detailed, so eloquent, that I was never allowed to play with May Ellen again.

My older sister, Caroline, did not take kindly to the news that it was actually me who was oldest. "You're not a person when you're an egg," she argued. "You don't know anything about the world. So it doesn't count." Then she told me that Walt Disney, the creator of some of my very favorite films, had frozen his corpse, was in fact lying on ice at that very moment in a locked freezer in Florida.

My younger sister, Bea, who was only two, didn't care about any of it until Caroline lay down on the floor, stiff as a board, eyes bulging, and pretended to be frozen and dead. Then Bea let out a single long wail and Caroline had to get up quickly to demonstrate that she was still alive while I made soothing noises and patted a steady rhythm into my little sister's back. My mother had no patience for crying and, if she had heard it, would have sent us mercilessly into the prickly front yard to keep an eye on each other while she locked herself in the house and took what she called a breather.

My father lived on the south side of the house. He entered through the back door and rarely saw my mother at all, except at meal times. "He'll never leave me," my mother said once. "He'd starve."

My father's side of the house was warm, full of ceramic bowls of fruit baking in the sun. Always the smell of rotting oranges, sweet and sickly. In the summers, he picked wildflowers and left them in jars on the windowsills, shedding petals and pollen until the water in the jars turned to a brown film. There was a sun porch tacked onto his side of the house, cold in the winter, hot in summer. The floor sloped away from the house, down towards the yard. It was covered in plastic stick-on tiles meant to look like slate. There were black curtains stapled to the window casings and a lock that bolted from the inside, since my father, who used the room as his studio, often hired nude models. The floors and shelves were covered in a mix of paints, turpentine, brushes, hammers, drills, extension cords. In his spare time, my father worked as a handyman. For Christmas, my mother had given him large rectangular magnets to stick to the side of his purple van. They said "Wilson Gratta, Handyman," and included the home phone number, the one that connected to the kitchen phone on my mother's side of the house.

We were not allowed on the porch where my father painted—none of us, not even our mother. My sisters and I had snuck in when my father wasn't home and seen for ourselves the reason why. There were white sheets over almost everything—the chairs, his easel—and pencil-drawn nudes tacked to the walls, taped to the blackout curtains. They all showed the same small, pale woman, bones protruding from her skin. In most of the images, she was turned away. My father seemed especially fixated on her vertebrae. In the sketches where she faced forward, he had taken his thumb and smudged out most of her face, like he had breathed too deeply and a gray wind had carried her away.

That was the secret, we figured. That he did not just hire nude models, but one in particular.

Because I knew what it felt like to be in love, because I had secrets of my own, I didn't hate my father for the time he spent locked up with that woman, Ava, drawing her naked body.

I was in love, more or less secretly, with Evan Barstow, a boy in Caroline's grade who had been struck by lightning and lived. She was in love with him too, but the important distinction was that I had been in love with him before the lightning strike, whereas she, along with most of the girls at school, hadn't been in love with Evan Barstow until after.

The lightning had come down on Evan's right shoulder, shot straight through him, singed off most of his hair, narrowly missed his heart, zipped through the sole of his right foot, and gone deep into the earth. The day after it happened, there was an article on the front page of the newspaper below a picture of Evan, shirtless, displaying a forked scar, a tangle of purple veins that spread over his shoulder and down the length of his torso. The paper said it was a miracle he had survived. "What did it feel like when the lightning hit?" the reporter had asked him, but Evan had only shrugged and said he couldn't remember. Caroline had researched lightning strikes on one of the library computers at school and informed me it felt like being punched hard in the stomach. I preferred to imagine it as an electric shock, a slow tingle that spread beneath the skin like a crack in a windshield.

My mother had always promised that the summer I turned twelve, I could have my very first bikini. Until then, she said, I would wear the faded blue one-piece

Speedo that Caroline had worn before me, and I would be grateful she didn't make me wear briefs and an oversized T-shirt, the way her mother had done to her. When that summer finally rolled around, though, my mother broke the news that we didn't have the money for silly things like new swimsuits. She was genuinely sorry. She said she knew what it felt like to want something and to be disappointed. Then, when I cried, she stopped feeling sorry and locked me out in the front yard. "How did you get to be such a spoiled brat?" she asked.

I stretched out on my back with a big lump in my throat, tears rolling down the sides of my cheeks, watering the grass. I prayed I would be struck by lightning too, and the papers would come to interview me, and I would tell them how my mother had locked me outdoors, put me in harm's way. I would show off my purple scar in a black bikini, a brand new one paid for by the newspaper. What I wouldn't give to have the same scar as Evan.

I looked to the sky, but it was a deep June blue. No clouds.

I wondered what Evan was doing, if he still felt pain or crackling electricity near his heart. Before he'd been struck, he'd had beautiful loose brown curls that fell around his face and had to be brushed constantly from his eyes. Now he was bald, with patches of pink scar tissue, and on the right side of his face he had only half of an eyebrow.

A leaf broke free from the big oak tree above me and floated down onto my stomach. Around the side of the house, I could hear music coming from my father's studio, loud jazz, the piercing notes of a trombone. Someone was singing along, maybe Ava.

After a while, my mother came outside and lay next to me on the lawn. She was sorry again, I could tell, but she didn't say anything at first. We looked up at the branches of the oak tree and listened to the music, the woman singing.

"You look nice in the blue swimsuit," she said after some time. I didn't respond. I knew it was a lie. I turned my head towards her and fixed my eyes on a point above her face, on one of the house's chipped red clapboards.

"What do you think about an Avon spa party?" she asked. "For your birthday this year. We can do pampering, makeovers, a nice dinner." She glanced at me. "You can invite boys to the dinner part if you'd like," she said. She was smiling. She could sense the cracks forming in my resolve. "Come on," she said, "we can pick out products in the living room." My mother led me back inside her half of the house. She shut the door, muffling the noise of the jazz music. The living room was the most cramped room in the house, the windows completely sealed off by boxes. A few small lamps set up on top of more boxes cast circles of dim orange light, deep blue shadows. My mother wiped dust off the tops of boxes with her hands, then handed them to me to open. "Try on anything you want," she said. She took a mirror compact out of her purse, helped me put on red lipstick and thick swoops of black eyeliner. She did her sales routine with me, like I was a paying customer. "And here," she said, unscrewing the cap from a tub of pale green mud, "we have a cleansing, firming seaweed mud mask." She let me stick my fingers in the mask, smooth and cold as cement.

Though I rarely ever saw Ava in person, every time that I did, she looked thinner. Mostly I spotted her coming and going through the doors of my father's sun porch studio. Once, she saw me bored in the front yard, tearing up fistfuls of clovers, and she stopped to tell me the heart-shaped ones were edible, that they had a pleasant, sour taste. Another time, when I had gone to my father's side of the house to hide from my mother, I walked in on Ava in the bathroom, sitting on the toilet with her blue jeans puddled up around her ankles and her knees like pink doorknobs on the white sticks that were her legs. She had let out a shriek and I closed the door quietly, as if nothing had happened, and retreated to my bedroom on my mother's side. I hardly knew Ava, and so, when I observed her getting thinner, at first I doubted myself. I snuck into my father's studio, wondering if I could see the change in the tacked-up drawings, and instead found that his entire artistic style and sensibility had changed. Now he drew Ava with thick lines, as a caricature of herself, so that her bones really did come out of her skin, her whole skeleton exposed. Not only that, but he had begun drawing her face like a tiny pin on top of her body in which, if I leaned up close, I could see grotesquely realistic features, her cracked lips and upturned nose. Her hair—in real life limp, white blond—flowed from her head in long tendrils that looped in and out of her ribs and seemed to grow in the direction of her heart.

My father's new drawings of Ava haunted me. I had nightmares about her white-blond hair wrapping around my skin, turning to bone and imprisoning me in her grasp. In other dreams, Ava got thinner and thinner until she was nearly flat, like folded paper, but her knees, round and pink, remained very large and clicked together when she walked. I tried to talk to Caroline about these dreams, about Ava, about our father's new style of drawing. Bold cartoon lines like he had finally figured something out, though what I couldn't say.

Caroline was annoyed. "I hate him," she said. "I hate him and I hate his drawings."

I was shocked. I reached instinctively for Bea, to calm her, to cover her ears, though she wasn't crying.

"Oh please," Caroline said, "Bea will find out someday and so will you. There's no money because all he does is waste his time drawing pictures of that woman. She's not even pretty." She paused, considered. "I bet plenty of men cheat on their wives," she said. "And the other way around, too. But most people have the decency to cover it up, to do it somewhere private where at least their kids can't see."

"Do you think they kiss?" I asked.

"Do you think they kiss?" she singsonged in a little girl voice. "Of course they kiss."

"They must be in love," I said, unsure of myself.

I had misspoken again. She was very sensitive about love, now that she and I were both in love with Evan. "You can't just throw the word around," she liked to say, whenever possible. "When I say it, I want it to really mean something." She claimed, too, that because she and Evan were in the same grade together, she had first dibs, and I couldn't have him at all, never mind how long I had loved him, never mind that my egg had been frozen longer than hers. It wasn't real, she said, that childish love I felt for him. It was called "infatuation," she explained, and that was what our father felt for Ava, too.

Still, because Caroline was experiencing real, true love, we hung around the community pool almost every afternoon that summer, our towels spread as near to Evan as possible, but slightly farther back, so that we could sit in the shade of the chain-link fence and watch him and Bea at the same time, without trouble, without giving ourselves away.

Before that summer, Caroline had never cared about owning a bikini. Instead, when she turned twelve, she had picked out a lime green tankini that showed only the smallest strip of belly. Now that there was no money for swimsuits of any kind, she had realized her mistake and compensated by rolling her tankini up farther over her stomach, into a makeshift bikini that was at least, she said, better looking than the old blue Speedo.

The pool was where we first saw Evan's lightning scar in person. For the first few days of summer, he never took off his T-shirt, and he wore a baseball cap to protect his newly bare head. Then, on a Tuesday afternoon late in June, he took off his hat, placed it carefully on top of his shoes, tugged his shirt over his head very slowly, like he was sunburnt and had to be careful not to touch his skin too forcefully with the cotton of his T-shirt. Caroline and I held our breath. The picture in the paper hadn't shown the yellow and green bruises that blossomed beneath the scar, blotting out some of the finer purple lines. We watched him walk slowly to the deep end of the pool, sit down on the concrete with his feet in the water, scooting forward until he slid, with barely a ripple, beneath the surface. I imagined that was the last of the electricity, that it crackled into the water and was gone from his body. I imagined the relief he must feel, cool water on his bruised, blistered skin.

Then, as if the whole neighborhood had been watching Evan, waiting for him to undress and slip into the water, people began to come from all sides of the pool, to crowd around his towel, to wait for him to resurface. He was down a long time, then came up only briefly for air before slipping back under. He wasn't swimming, exactly, he was just going up and down, dunking himself over and over. He only climbed out of the pool when a cloud passed over the sun and, from the depths, he must have seen the water darken a shade or two, must have felt the chill. Then he hoisted himself over the edge—his hands, a leg, another leg. No one said a word, no one even looked in his direction. He returned to his towel amid a stunned silence, all of us sneaking glances at the spot where the lightning had entered his body. Nobody said anything at all until Bea, arms fat and swaddled in inflatable floaties, pointed and shrieked, "What's that?" Caroline slapped a hand over our sister's mouth. I gave her a soothing rub on her back. Bea's eyes were wide, tracing the yellows, greens, purples of Evan's skin. She looked at me, at Caroline. Unable to speak, she began to cry.

"It's okay," I muttered. "Don't worry, it's okay."

But everything was not okay. A girl named Eliza, a grade ahead of Caroline, broke from the ranks of the crowd and approached Evan. She was wearing an orange bikini the color of a monarch butterfly, her skin a dark, polished bronze. "Does it hurt?" she asked. Evan shrugged. She smiled. "Can I touch it then?" He nodded and, right there in front of our eyes, she reached out her hand and he let her trace her fingers all down his chest, wincing as she brushed his bruises.

Not long after I found my father's horrible new drawings, I learned that Ava really was sick. I heard my mother on the phone with her sister, saying that she and my father had begun covering some of Ava's medical bills. "All of them, actually, in one way or another," she said. "Posing for Wilson is the only job she has."

I was in the living room, all the lamps turned on, rummaging through the open boxes of Avon goods for my birthday party. I had gotten it into my head to hand out gift bags to my guests, something that I had seen done at other birthday parties. I was looking for Avon trinkets small enough, cheap enough that my mother would allow me to give them away when I heard her explaining that, because of Ava, money was very tight. "But I suppose it's important," she said. "I suppose it's not something that can be avoided."

I wasn't sure what kind of sick Ava was, but finally I had the confirmation that she really was losing weight, that things were bad. I had the confirmation, too, from my father, who had such dark circles beneath his eyes that they looked bruised, who had stopped sketching graphite on paper and begun to put the paint straight onto Ava's body instead.

Still, my birthday party approached, planned amid the chaos of Ava dying, of my father slowly losing his mind. My mother, in a frenzy, ordered more makeup that she couldn't sell. The house was darker, more cramped than ever. She sent us to the front yard more and more often, not because we misbehaved or because Bea cried, but because there was no room for us in any of the common spaces. "Get out," she would say, whenever the crush of space began to overwhelm her. "Get out, get out," and she would send us into the afternoon sun, sometimes with a pitcher of lemonade or apple juice, mixed from a can of frozen slush and cut with too much water.

In the front yard, we could hear my father in his studio. He had begun to play polka music while he painted, very loud, so that when I listened my heart began to stutter out

of rhythm. Ava was in the studio with him only sometimes, only when she could be. When she wasn't, my
father tried painting from memory, but it didn't go well
for him and from the yard we often heard him giving up,
throwing his brushes against the windows.

It was during another morning like this, sitting in the
grass and pulling up the heart-shaped clovers, listening to
polka, to my father's scuffles with himself, that Caroline
looked at me and asked, "Do you think Mom hopes Ava
will die?"

I'd never thought about that before, about our mother
as evil, but in that moment I got an image, just for a second, of her lying in her cold, dark bedroom, burgundy
hair splayed out on the pillow, eyes closed and wishing,
really wishing for Ava to die. "Of course not," I said, rolling my eyes at Caroline, but inside I was busy imagining
my own life without Ava, wondering if I, like my mother,
might have a streak of evil.

Another important thing happened during that time. On
one of our afternoons at the pool, Evan came up to me—
came up to Caroline, Bea, and me but spoke only to me—
to ask if I would like to go on a walk with him someday.
He knew a better swimming spot, a shady stretch of river
without a chain-link fence, without—he eyed Bea—kids
who peed in the water.

"A walk?" I asked. I thought I hadn't heard him right. I
stopped myself from adding, "With me?"

Caroline, of course, was livid. As soon as I had agreed to go to the river the following Friday, she snatched up her things and said in a voice that was not her own, "Well, we have to be going, can't waste the whole day paddling around in the pool." Bea, who hadn't had a chance to go in the water yet, began to cry, and Caroline looked at her like she wished she could lock her out in the front yard. "You better finish crying by the time we get home," she said, hoisting Bea onto her hip and heading for the gate without stopping to wait for me.

"Bye," I said to Evan and hustled after Caroline, though I wanted to stay, to look at the whole mess of his scar, to brush my fingers over his chest like Eliza had done, wearing her orange bikini, radiant in the sun.

Even with Caroline scowling and slapping her bare feet as hard as she could against the hot pavement, and even with Bea, whose cries, unattended to, had turned into chest-rattling screams, I was ecstatic. Buoyant. I was going to the river with Evan. The river was where the older kids went, the ones in high school, the ones who drank beer in the sun and jumped from high rocks, holding hands, shrieking all the way down. I had been to the river, of course, but only ever with my mother, who wore a swimsuit that looked like a dress, who never let me go beyond where I could touch, who gripped my hand tightly and shouted, "Idiot could've died!" every time one of the high-schoolers leapt from the cliffs and landed, with a splash, in one of the deep green pools.

At home, my mother was vacuuming with a ferocious rage directed at the uneven floorboards, at the dusty, hard-to-reach corners. "Six friends," she said, as soon as she saw me. "I told you six friends only."

"Okay," I said. I could hardly hear her. I already felt far away, on the ledges above the river, spending the afternoon with a boy she didn't even know.

"I don't know what you think this is," she went on, shouting over the noise of the vacuum. "A restaurant? I can hardly afford to feed you three, let alone all your friends. Let alone your father, who I would never see otherwise." She placed the suction over a daddy longlegs and sucked it into the bag of dirt and hair inside the machine.

Caroline turned on her heel and marched up to her room, leaving me with Bea, who had quieted down but was still sniffling, building up the energy to cry some more. My mother jammed the vacuum against the wooden trim along the bottom edge of the wall. "And here I am," she said, "giving away makeup that I should be selling. Putting lipstick on little girls." She was talking like I wasn't there anymore, like I couldn't hear. I turned and went through the hallway into my father's side of the house, afraid of hearing her say something she shouldn't, afraid of losing the little pulse of happiness that was still beating inside of me. I left Bea behind, too. Let my mother take care of her. Let her lock her in the front yard.

From the hallway, I could hear that Ava was in my father's studio. They were listening to oldies—*shake, rattle, and roll*—and they were both singing. I wondered if I had ever heard him so happy, doubted he was sketching anything at all, had even bothered to pick up a pencil today. I thought the laugh he used with her was different from the one he used with me, but if I thought too hard about it, I couldn't remember the laugh he used with me. I only had vague, noiseless memories, and they seemed far away, from when I was very young. Walking to the post office, being pushed on the swings, eating orange Popsicles that were sold in twos, frozen together so they had to be snapped apart like the wishbone in a turkey.

Just before I left to meet Evan at the river, Caroline emerged from her room. She had been crying, her eyes puffy and pink, some of the tendrils of hair around her temples damp and curly from the way her tears had rolled off the sides of her face. She was holding her lime green tankini. Very solemnly, she handed it to me. For a minute, she seemed incapable of speaking. Then she said, "You look awful in the blue Speedo," turned back into her room, and slammed the door.

"Thank you!" I yelled at her closed door. In the bathroom, I swapped swimsuits. The tankini was a size or two too big—it bunched under my shorts and the straps kept slipping off my shoulders—but it was bright and new looking and it made me feel good.

I realized too late that there were a lot of things I didn't know about going on a date. Was there an obligation to dress a certain way? To say certain things? Was a kiss guaranteed or did I have to do certain things to ensure that it happened? And how did a kiss work, exactly? Had Evan kissed someone before? Was that the kind of thing you had to ask early on or the kind of thing you had to wait to find out, even if it might hurt you? And was the kiss meant to come at the end of the date, or was that logistically impossible, given that our parents would be arriving to pick us up? I wondered if even Caroline knew these things. I was almost certain that she didn't.

My father drove me to the river in his purple van with the magnets on the sides. It was the first time I had been alone with him in months, and I found that we had very little to talk about. When I looked at the side of his face, gaunt, scruffy, my mind ran through a catalogue of all the things I knew about him, about his life, and there was nothing, really, that I was allowed to say. I thought about Ava on the toilet. I thought about my father loving her.

"Did you and Mom always live on separate sides of the house?" I asked.

My father turned down the radio. It had been playing a talk show, something where one man spoke in many different voices. "What was that?"

"Did you and Mom always live on separate sides of the house?"

He didn't answer right away, just worked his jaw like he was chewing on the question. "No," he said finally. "Not always. But almost always."

"Did you ever draw Mom?"

"Yes," my father said, "once. She didn't like it."

"She wouldn't, would she?"

"No," my father said, "she's not like that."

We pulled down a little dirt road that opened up into a sandy parking lot. "Well," he said, "your date awaits."

I looked out the window of the van. There was nobody in the parking lot. Just a little path that wound its way through the trees to the edge of the river.

"Did she not like how she looked in the drawing? Or was it that she didn't like sitting for so long?"

My father shook his head. "I don't know," he said, but he had a faraway look. I wasn't sure he'd heard my question at all.

I found Evan down by the river, skipping stones. His scar rippled when he slung his arm back, flicked his wrist. He had his headphones on and hadn't heard me approach, so I stood for a minute just watching him. It was like I was at the pool again with Caroline, strategically laying out our towels. If Bea were here, she'd take one look at Evan's damaged skin and cry. I thought of the bolt of lightning at the exact moment it struck Evan in the shoulder, wondered if he'd lit up blue.

"Hey," I said finally, but he couldn't hear me over the buzz of his music, leaking from his headphones. "Hey," I said again. He flicked another rock into the river. This one didn't skip, just made one clumsy splash and sank.

"Son of a bitch," Evan said to himself. "Son of a goddamn bitch."

I waited another minute. I didn't want him to know I'd seen his failed skipping stone or heard the way he spoke when he thought he was alone. Then I stepped closer, tapped him once on the shoulder, the smooth one without the scar.

He jumped. "Jesus," he said. "Hey."

I had never been to the river on my own. We waded into the water together, walking upstream over rocks slick with algae. When I stumbled and slipped, Evan put out his arm to catch me and then didn't let go. He was so close, I was afraid he could hear how nervous I was, and I tried to slow down my breathing, to make it come out in an even, shallow beat.

"Where did you learn to skip rocks?" I asked, but Evan just shrugged.

The water got deeper, and in the shade of the trees it was sometimes so dark and murky that I couldn't see my own toes.

"Where are we going?" I asked. Evan shrugged again, moved his hand down my arm and wiggled his fingers between mine. I was quiet then. I felt lightheaded from breathing in so little air.

Upstream, the river widened. He led me up a path through the trees to a spot above the water, a rocky cliff covered in a stringy network of roots.

"What are we doing?" I asked, and finally, Evan spoke. "Jumping."

I peered over the ledge. Black water. I heard my mother's voice. "*Idiot could've died!*"

Evan grinned at me. "We'll go together," he said. He was still holding my hand in his. With my other hand, I hiked up the tankini bottoms and prayed they wouldn't fall off when I hit the water. We stepped closer to the ledge, our toes hanging off the rock into thin air. "Ready?" His voice was low in his throat. He sounded bored.

"Ready," I said, felt my arm jerk, and was tugged over the edge. For a moment, I was falling, watching the tree branches, the stripes on the rocks where the water levels had risen, then sunk. I sent up one quick, final prayer about the tankini and about not crushing my skull on some gray rock and floating downstream, bloated and purple, for my mother to find and pull out of the river. Then I hit the water hard with my forearms, a massive slap, and sank into a haze of bubbles, water filling up my nose. Evan let go of my hand. I stayed under until the pain was gone from my arms, then splashed to the surface, coughing. River water, now warm, ran through my nose and down the back of my throat. I held in the urge to gag. My swimsuit had stayed put, thank God. Evan surfaced just a moment later, his bald head shooting through the water like a seal's. He was panting and laughing.

"You really like me, don't you?" he said, looking me right in the eye.

"So what?" I said, my skin turning hot.

"So nothing," he said, slipping back underwater and blowing bubbles with his nose.

Later, sitting on the rocks in the sun, Evan showed me how to skip stones. I was no good at it, and neither was he, but he said, "These rocks are all wrong. All wrong."

I closed my eyes into the sun and imagined us back in the water, sinking in the bubbles. I imagined Evan as my boyfriend, which he maybe was and maybe wasn't. "My boyfriend, Evan," I imagined saying. "My boyfriend, Evan, was struck by lightning."

When I opened my eyes again, I invited him to my birthday party. I had already invited more people than my mother had allowed.

"Cool," he said, chucking another rock into the river and swearing under his breath. "We'll see."

When the day of my birthday finally came, very little went according to plan. First, the guests were late. I sat in the kitchen with my mother, arranging and rearranging a row of lipsticks. She had gotten her nails done for the occasion, painted a shade of brown called "Raisin," and tapped them against the counter with increasing speed so that my heart matched their pace, then rocketed to keep up. Finally she said, "Well, let me put your face on anyway," and began smoothing creams and powders over my skin, not touching any of the brushes or sponges she had laid out on the table, using her cold, dry hands instead.

The first knock surprised us both. We jumped. My mother was in the middle of applying mascara with a little black wand, and she flicked it up over my eyelid, leaving wet, black stripes. She handed me a compact mirror and a crumpled tissue. "Spit on it," she said, "and clean that mess up." She hurried to the front door. I heard voices, shoes being kicked off. The mascara smudged around my eye like a bruise. My guests, it seemed, had carpooled to the party. They were already talking, giggling about jokes told in the car. I sat on the kitchen stool, skin powdered white, one eye smudged a deep, smoky gray, and tried to pick up the pieces of their conversation. It was confusing, jumping back and forth.

A kiss. Someone had been kissed. My mother kept interjecting, "take a seat, think about what look you want." Someone mentioned a scar. "We can do natural browns. We can do girly pinks," my mother said, like she was deaf to the conversation going on around her. Something cold was spreading down from my throat, deep into my stomach. My heart had slowed to a steady, loud thumping, a beat pounding in my ears. "Yes, his scar," someone was saying. "She touched his scar." I scratched at the smear around my eye, trying to take the makeup off with my fingernail. I felt sick to my stomach. "She said the kiss was pretty good," someone said, "but how could it not be?" I tried to make eye contact with my mother, but she was hovering over the lipsticks, still rattling off looks. "Movie star glam," she said to no one in particular. "80s color pop." My eye was irritated now, scratched red and raw. "Hello," I said, my voice small and petty. "I look like a monster, can somebody help me?"

Finally, my mother turned towards me. "Oh," she said. "Right." She put some oil on a cotton ball and swabbed at my skin. She reapplied the mascara. Added eyeliner. Sprayed my whole face with something she called a setting spray. When she was done, she held up a mirror. "Movie star glam," she said. "You look like a young lady." I rolled my eyes at her, but I did look good. Like a different person. Better than usual. Evan would see me, I thought, and he would regret whatever kiss he'd had without me.

The girls, my friends, didn't take the makeovers as seriously as I had. They chose bright neon colors and laughed as my mother applied them, so their faces shook and the makeup didn't go on in straight lines. Caroline came down with Bea, and my mother gave Caroline a makeover, even put a little lipstick on Bea, who smeared the red color all over her face and roared like a beast. We drank juice spritzers and painted each other's nails. When they were dry, my mother shooed us into the yard so she could make dinner. We sat on the scrubby grass. There were no sounds from my father's studio, just the cool silence of the yard. A girl named Lise said she was hungry. "The heart-shaped clovers are edible," I said, and ate one just to prove my point. Ava had been right, it was sour, a bit like a lime. I smiled while I chewed to emphasize that the clover really was edible, I wasn't making this up. Lise plucked one from the ground and stuck it in her mouth. "Better than nothing," she said. The other girls began picking clovers too, roaming across the lawn in their search. All of us on our knees, trying not to smudge our lipstick, eating handfuls of the lawn.

After that, things only got worse. Unlike the girls, the boys showed up slowly, in separate cars, carrying small, wrapped gifts. They kept to themselves, in a tight huddle, as they though they didn't know any of us girls. No one said a word about our makeovers except for one boy, Adam, who climbed out of his mother's car and said, "What did you do to your faces?" I hadn't planned anything for us to do before dinner, an oversight on my part, and when I looked around at my classmates and friends, milling about in the yard, it occurred to me that none of them knew how much time I spent out here, sitting on moss and twigs, doing nothing at all. Caroline and Bea had stayed inside to help with dinner, but I wished for my sisters now, even Bea, who knew how to sit next to me in silence, or look at the sky, or tap the ground to the rhythm of dad's polka music, rolling our eyes at our whole existence.

Evan was the last to arrive, twenty-five minutes late. Dinner still wasn't ready. He hadn't brought a wrapped gift, just a card in a red envelope. I took it from him, thanked him, and when he wasn't looking I sniffed it to see if it smelled like him, but it smelled plain, like paper and glue.

I led Evan into the yard. "I had fun at the river the other day," I said.

"Yeah."

Lise called out to him, "Evan! Come pick clovers with me. Lucy says you can eat them."

I turned red, stopped walking. Evan walked to Lise, and I stood alone in the yard looking at the sticks, at the moss, at the two big trees. I thought, for some reason, about my mother, waking up alone to put on mascara, smudge gold eye shadow into the creases of her eyelids, pat a pinkish brown powder onto the apples of her wrinkled cheeks, careful not to smudge her face as she pulled on one of her old turtlenecks. The house cold. Cardboard boxes stacked against the walls.

For dinner, she'd roasted a chicken, made pesto pasta with cream, and laid out yellow and red cherry tomatoes cut in half with their insides exposed. She had pushed together the kitchen and dining room tables, covered them with a burgundy cloth, and lit several large, white candles. There was music on the stereo in the other room, not my father's jumpy polka music but smooth piano, something that sounded like it was from another time. She ushered us into the house like a host in a fancy restaurant. "Your table is right this way," she said. She had changed into a black turtleneck and black sweatpants, so in the dim lighting it almost looked like she'd gotten dressed up. She led me to the head of the table and pulled out a chair for me. "The guest of honor," she said, then left the room. She, Caroline, and Bea were eating in the living room. Caroline had been invited, but she was avoiding Evan. "He's a bad seed," she'd said earlier that day, sounding a million years old, as though she hadn't spent half the summer pining for him at the community pool.

When everyone got settled, we looked over the food.

"What's this green stuff?" Evan asked, then interrupted when I tried to explain what pesto was, poking his finger into the dish and saying, "Sounds weird to me." The rest of the boys cackled. One named Liam said, "Green slop!" and poked his fingers into the bowl too.

Then Lise said, "I heard you had a good time with Eliza the other day," and things got even worse. I didn't wait for Evan's answer. "I have to go pee," I announced and ran out of the room.

In the living room, Caroline had her plate piled high with pasta. She was mixing in the chicken and tomatoes with her fork, using the strength of her entire arm. Bea had creamy pesto smeared across her lips and a dot of green on the tip of her nose. She was smiling and babbling to herself. "Yes," she kept saying, "Yes, yes, okay."

I hovered in the doorway. "Come eat with us," I said. "Please?"

Caroline smiled into her pasta. My mother shook her head, said they were all settled in. She promised they would join us for cake and that she would try to track down my father too.

But when cake time rolled around, when I had endured dinner, when Caroline had pulled up a chair next to me and rested her head on my shoulder in a gesture of forgiveness, my father was nowhere to be found. My mother was nervous, scrunching the sleeves of her shirt up over her elbows, tugging them back down again and squeezing at her wrists. "I guess we'll have to start without him," she said finally, after Liam had begun to kick Evan beneath the table, after Lise had started yawning and pushed her empty plate out of the way to rest her head on her placemat. My mother went into the kitchen to get the cake, brought it out with the candles blazing, dripping wax onto the buttercream frosting. She sang in her scratchy, loud voice and gestured at everyone else to sing with her, to raise their voices. Lise didn't take her head off the table, just eyed the cake with the eye that was angled up towards the ceiling.

"Make a wish," my mother said, and I closed my eyes, squeezed them shut. For Evan again at the river, for my father to paint nice things, to love my mother again. I blew out the candles before I had picked something. When I opened my eyes, my father was standing in the doorway. My mother, who had been about to help me cut the cake, was standing with the knife extended towards me like a threat. Evan, Caroline, my party guests, were all looking at him. He was bright red, and at first I thought he was lit up by the aftereffect of the candle glow. I blinked in his direction. My mother handed me the knife, shook it in my direction, impatient for me to take it. "Cut the cake," she said. My father, I saw, was crying. My mother moved towards him, across the room. She put a hand on his back and pushed him into the hallway.

Evan had his eyes fixed on the table now, thinking hard about something, the purple scar creeping up the side of his neck and pulsing. I looked down at my cake, at the candles still dripping wax, brought the knife down and cut the first slice, a big slice, larger than my mother would have allowed. I passed it to Caroline. The table was stone silent. In the hallway, my father was making choking noises. Too much air to his lungs, then not enough.

The party ended badly. My mother came back and announced that Ava was dead. I kept slicing cake, but nobody knew if they were allowed to eat or not.

After that, my mother began staying on my father's side of the house. Caroline, Bea, and I were alone with the boxes. I had more dreams about my father's drawings of Ava, with her hair winding through my bones.

One day, sitting on the lawn, Caroline said, "Evan Barstow had kind of ratty old swim trunks, didn't he?"

"Yeah," I said, "he did."

Autumn came, then winter. My father locked himself in his studio. We heard music—horrible, ear-splitting opera—but we almost never saw him. Caroline told Bea he didn't eat anymore, that he lived off paint fumes, that this was why he could never leave his studio. Bea cried when she heard that, and then calmed herself down and began to sniff the air for funny smells, convinced she could live off them too. When someone called about handyman work, my mother answered the calls herself, driving my father's van with the big magnets to strangers' houses, trying to sell lipstick while she plunged a toilet or fixed a leak.

For the first time in my life, the big red house felt too large, like a labyrinth that circled round and round. My mother turned the thermostat up on her side, tried to lure my father back with comfortable, familiar things. She had always liked her space, but now it seemed to make her anxious. From time to time she would scoop Bea into her arms, make shushing noises and hum, even when Bea wasn't crying. "Where's your father?" she would say in a soothing voice. "Where is he?"

When my father wasn't locked in his studio, my parents sat huddled together in the living room on his side of the house, making notes on a pad of yellow paper. My mother shooed us out of the room when we were noisy, when we asked what they were working on. It was November now—too cold for the scrubby yellow lawn—so we were exiled to other parts of the house instead, to our bedrooms, to the dark rooms stacked with boxes. We lay on the floor and looked at the shadowy ceilings, at cobwebs, at each other. I asked Caroline if she thought our parents loved each other again and she said they had never stopped. I didn't understand. We recalled meals my mother had made, some of the best, the ones that had drawn our father out of his studio and into the dining room. Chicken wrapped in thick strips of bacon, peach pie with yellow scoops of French vanilla ice cream. Our mother hardly ever cooked anymore. We ate oranges out of the refrigerator and shrink-wrapped meals that could be heated in the microwave.

Once, I worked up the courage to ask Caroline about Evan. I told her about the river, how we'd held hands when we jumped from the cliffs. "What do you think happened?"

I asked her, and she explained that boys' brains matured differently, more slowly. His was still mush. The lightning strike, she said, had probably warmed it up and made it even softer. Then she thought for a while and said, "Maybe it'll always be mush." She wasn't teasing. Some people, she explained, love you forever, no matter what. And some people love little parts of you, or a picture of you, like a photograph of an old relative who you don't remember but who you have to love anyway.

In February, my mother announced my father's first gallery show. It was to be held at the local community college, in a hallway that they had rented out for two and a half weeks. The show was called *For Ava*. My mother's lips twitched when she said the name. I wondered if the show title was her idea, and not my father's. I wondered if the show itself was her own idea, crafted as she went on handyman house calls, as she applied golden powder to her crinkled eyelids each morning, as she sent us kids off to school, to the yard, to the other rooms.

I hadn't seen any of my father's work since the day I'd snuck in and seen the horrible portrait of Ava, with her bones exposed and her hair winding its way through her ribcage, so when we arrived at the side entrance to the arts and sciences building, I was nervous. I was wearing a big blue winter coat, and underneath I felt sweaty, like if I took it off there might be wet spots on the fabric of my dress. My father looked nervous too. He was skinny, and his dress clothes hung from him in funny ways. He was pale. At home, I had overheard my mother offer to put a bit of blush on him. "Just to give you some color," she had said, but he had refused.

The hallway with my father's paintings was crowded with students. They all looked very beautiful to me. There was one girl, in particular, who I could not stop staring at. She had her dark hair pulled back in a loose ponytail, messy, with strands falling out of the hair tie, framing her face. She was wearing a tight black skirt, like she had started to get dressed up, and an old ratty T-shirt, like she had given up trying. She reminded me of my mother, how she worked very hard on certain aspects of her appearance but always wore the same pair of green sweatpants with elastic around the ankles. This girl was young, though, and seemed happy. She was laughing. She knew, I think, that she was beautiful. I caught my mother staring at her too, maybe thinking the same thing as me, that this girl could've been her, thirty years ago. There must've been a time, I realized, that she had looked at my father's paintings and fallen in love with him.

My mother had posted flyers around campus advertising the art show, which is why the space was so packed with students. According to Caroline, the flyers said, "Free drinks and refreshments." Most of the students milling around in the hallway were holding little plastic cups of cheap red wine and smacking their lips as they stared up at my father's paintings, thinking god knows what.

What I was thinking was: If my mother could afford all that wine, she sure could've afforded to buy me a bikini.

Although the hallway was a straight shot between one end of the building and the other, the show, *For Ava*, was designed in a circle. We walked down one side of the hallway, made a U-turn at the doorway, and came back up the other side. First came my father's smudged graphite drawings of Ava. Ava with no face or no feet, soft gray, disappearing. For the first time, I could see the slow steps of his progression into the horrible, bony portraits that I had dreamt about for weeks. The lines became stronger, Ava's legs stretching longer, thinner. He drew her skull on a smudged, realistic body. Then he drew all of her bones, emerging at once. The college students liked these ones. They gathered around and looked at Ava's exposed bones, muttering and smiling with each other. The girl who reminded me of my mother made a noise of pity in the back of her throat, like she'd seen a wounded animal. At the end of the hallway was an abrupt change. As Caroline and I made our way down the second wall, we saw no more pencil drawings. There were photographs now. Ava sitting naked on a chair, covered in paint. Our father had put purple and gray all over her face, smudging her features again, smoothing her out. I looked at her knees in the photos, the same knees I had seen when I'd walked in on her using the bathroom. Pink and round, like doorknobs. There were yellow fingerprints on one of her thighs that I tried not to look at, because I knew who they belonged to. My mother looked for a long time at this series. The nude photos. I don't know if she saw the fingerprints. Caroline didn't say anything about them either, just slid along to the last series, paintings done from memory after Ava's death.

These were the worst ones, because they were not very good. Once, my father had driven us to New York City and taken us to see some contemporary art in a museum. We had overheard a man saying to his girlfriend, "Well if that's art, then I'm an artist," and Caroline and I had found it very funny. At home, we made a game of who could draw the ugliest drawing and still get our father to hang it with a magnet on the fridge.

When I saw my father's final paintings of Ava, I thought: If this is art, then I'm an artist. Then I felt guilty. I knew these paintings had been hard for him, even if all he'd managed to get on the canvas were big strokes of purple and gray. One canvas was covered in a solid color, a pale, dirty yellow, and was titled, *Ava's hair*. Another, *Ava's Chapped Lips*, was the frosted pink of a drowned woman's mouth. It was awful looking at her like this, broken up into pieces. I thought of making a painting like this for Evan, a dark bloody purple called *Evan's scar*.

We had to stay until the end of the reception, when students began to filter out and a custodian came in and turned out most of the lights. My father looked exhausted. My mother sent us girls to pick up the plastic cups, stained with traces of wine, that the students had dropped on the floor. She sat with my father on two metal folding chairs near the doorway. They held hands. "You really captured her," I heard my mother say to him, and my father didn't say anything at all.

•

That was the last winter we spent in the big red house with the scrubby lawn. In the spring, my parents moved us across the country. "A fresh start," my mother said, but didn't add that the fresh start was for my father, who had sold some of his drawings, then bought them all back at double the price and buried them in the front yard under the clover.

One of my final memories from that house is coming home after my father's gallery reception, the remnants of the wine that my mother poured into coffee mugs, even for Caroline and me, who had never tasted wine before. How black the wine looked in the bottom of my mug. And when I try too hard to think about that home, split into halves, I remember it in pieces of distilled color: red house, yellow lawn, green river.

Ava's pink knees.

Evan's purple scar.

My blue swimsuit.